Other books by the author

The Tyranny of Questions (Unicorn Press)
Re-Write Men
Vocation

A Postcard from the Delta

Michael Gaspeny

Livingston Press

University of West Alabama

UWA
The UNIVERSITY of
WEST ALABAMA

ISBN 13: 978-1-60489-332-8, trade paper
ISBN 13: 978-1-60489-333-5, e-book
Library of Congress Control Number: 2022942111
Printed on acid-free paper.
Printed in the United States of America by
Publishers Graphics
Typesetting and page layout: Cassidy Pedram
Proofreading: Brooke Barger, Annsley Johnsey
Cover art, design, and layout: Joe Taylor
Cover photo of Mississippi John Hurt,
courtesy Smithsonian Museum
Author photo: Lee Zacharias

Acknowledgments:
"Seabirds" was excerpted in *Brilliant Corners: A Journal of Jazz and Literature* (Summer, 2019). Thanks to Sascha Feinstein, editor.
"Crossroads" appeared in *Embark: A Literary Journal for Novelists* (Issue 8, 2019). Thanks to Ursula DeYoung, editor.

first edition
6 5 4 3 2 1

Table of Contents

To my pal, the triple-threat author Steve Cushman,

who rescued this book from dust bunnies in my study closet

Hello

When everything is gone, what do you make out of nothing? That's the fix my blues heroes faced, and my trouble now. Every day I go to Howlin' Wolf, Muddy Waters, and Robert Johnson like a fundamentalist studies the Bible. Their music is sacred to me. I know it's 2000, the new millennium, and I'm 19 and supposed to like rap, country, alt rock, or head-banging music, but for me the rock of ages is the blues, and I like to draw my power from the source.

I need the music more than ever. Up until three months ago, I was a high school football star with a steady girlfriend, high grades, and a commitment to his community. I was popular, even admired. I'm Johnny Spink, and I used to live in Spinkville, Arkansas, an Ozark town named for my ancestors. Now I'm a long way from home, staying with my Uncle Roy in Islamorada, Florida and dragging toward graduation at Coral Shores High School. A scar runs down the left side of my face from the corner of my eye to the jaw. It looks like a long, ragged strip of dirty pink bubblegum. So far I've resisted seeing a plastic surgeon. Although the scar is ugly and humiliating, it guarantees people will avoid me, and I want privacy at this time in my life. I'm tired of hearing other people talk (except for Mr. Futrelle, whose story plays like a movie in my mind during bad times). The scar keeps essentials in front of me. Maybe farther down the road, when I grasp my lessons, I'll have my face repaired.

I had to leave Spinkville last Thanksgiving after I walked down the driveway, shaking the sleep from my head, to fetch *The Mountain Eagle* from its orange mailbox tube and found what looked like an old, gnawed boot. When I grabbed it, my fingers felt something slimy—bones, mangled, and stinking! Bile rose in my throat. Those bones used to walk and run, before they were twisted and hacked away. I slung the foot to the ground and lurched to the porch, tasting acid. My right hand felt contaminated. I yelled to Dad.

He rushed out, straightening his thick glasses, and looked

where I pointed. "My God, Johnny!" he shouted. "They won't leave you alone! You tried to tell the truth and look what you're getting! That's it! I'm calling Ed Sellers." He was our sheriff.

Since the Esmeraldo game the previous Friday, I had received threatening phone calls and poison pen letters from an array of haters. In a sense, the foot was my morning news. It could have been mine. Last fall, I enraged Arkansans from many corners of life. For a brief time, across the state, I was notorious. Ministers and leaders of racial organizations scorned me on TV, slanting statements I had made to the media during a post-game interview.

I rushed inside, washed my stinking hands in steaming water twice and doused them with rubbing alcohol. I brushed my teeth to drive the sick taste from my mouth, the toothpaste almost gagging me. Away from the football field, I was squeamish. What scared me wasn't slasher flicks, but real-life horror in the headlines every day and the racial injustice I had studied in a pre-college course at the University of Arkansas. There I saw a picture of Emmett Till's mauled corpse in his coffin and film of Rodney King being clubbed and clubbed. I learned that plantation owners had slit the Achilles tendons of slaves attempting to run away. Our text at the university contained a photo of a mob posing with a lynching victim it had mutilated. The gathering was a festive family affair, with mothers holding picnic baskets and big-eyed kids fascinated by the dangling man. The picnickers had complexions like mine. It horrified me that during the era of segregation, when many monstrous acts were committed against black citizens in my home state, the foot on my lawn could have belonged to Mr. Futrelle, the man I call Mr. F, the man I admire more than anyone in the world.

I put the toothbrush down. My mouth stung. A car surged up the driveway. From the front door, I saw Dad and Ed Sellers inspecting the foot. Ed slipped on latex gloves and slid the foot into an evidence bag. As Ed drove off, Dad said, "We're getting you out of here today!" On the two-day drive to Uncle Roy's place in the Keys, the foot lay at the edge of my mind like roadkill on the wayside. Just before Christmas, forensics experts in Little Rock determined it was a paw that once belonged to a black bear.

But that didn't cleanse my memory or keep me from thinking about the bear. I avoid reminders of mutilation, including the meat section at Payfair and the marinas at dusk when the guide boats return with their hauls. Proud anglers pose for pictures under their catch impaled on spiked racks. Then mates clean the fish, knives flashing, and flip slimy scraps to herons and egrets. I watched that ritual once, for about twenty seconds, before I rushed

Michael Gaspeny

from the dock. A few months ago, it would have thrilled me to be smiling in one of those photos. But that was in a different life. Now I know what it's like to get caught and cut.

Fortunately, my reputation has not followed me to Florida. Down here in the manana-land of the Keys, where everything can wait except fishing, I'm just the silent outsider with the weird scar who sticks to the back of the room and the palm shadows along the Overseas Highway. Even so, sometimes I have a fugitive's dread. What if someone discovers my secret, and the slurs start again? I have been called everything from a "wigger" (white nigger, in case you didn't know) to a bigot. I have been attacked by the NAACP and defended by Black Muslims.

I stay in a small apartment downstairs from Uncle Roy, the only person in the Sunshine State who knows what sent me here. He's a tight-lipped fishing guide, gone before sunrise and often at night. He looks in on me every few days, but mostly he lets me keep to myself, which is the lifestyle he practices. Roy broke out of society's maze long ago. Born in the mountains with a passion for fishing, he came to Islamorada, which the Chamber of Commerce, with good reason, calls "The Sport Fishing Capital of the World."

When I lived in the mountains, I loved to fish, too, especially with Mr. F, but here in anglers' paradise, I've lost my enthusiasm. Back in December, Roy took me fishing for bonefish and tarpon; even though he released our catches, it disturbed me to jerk the fish out of their element, and I asked to go back to shore. Maybe for the first time in my life, I know exactly what I need, and that's to leave fish and people alone. Writing is a safe way to create sympathetic company at a distance. Although I'm imagining you, your presence is real. I hope you'll hear me out.

Roy is my mother's brother. She's been gone about twelve years now, not dead, as far as I know, but departed, a fault-finding alcoholic who ended her connection with both sides of the family. We all disappointed her. I don't miss her outbursts, but I would like to know where she is. When I was little, my parents were drunks. They drank like drains. Before dinner, Dad cracked beers and Mom popped wine corks; afterward, ice burst from trays and rattled in glasses for the nightly visit by Jack Daniels, the only taste they shared. At our house, bottles chimed and glugged. Most of the time, they held off arguing until they thought I was asleep. Why were they drinking? Dad had inherited Ozark Poultry, the largest employer in Spinkville and a business he hated. Mom, detesting our drab town, took such lengthy trips that one became lasting.

Otherwise, I had the happy existence of a well-off boy who

could lug a football. Folks in Spinkville loved me, and I thought I loved them. Dad entered rehab, joined AA, sold the poultry plant, and became mayor. He and I lived as we pleased in the neglected rooms of our ancestral home on a hill above town square. Despite these blessings, one side of me must have sensed that trouble (or real life) lay just ahead, because the first time I heard the blues, the music grabbed me. I was easing the dial around my radio, hoping to pick up a football game, when I hit this growling singer backed by a band that sounded like an amplified tool box being shaken up and down. The song was Howlin' Wolf's "Smokestack Lightning." His ferocious groan and those guitars clanging like radiators split me in two. I had no idea what smokestack lightning was or what the words meant, but, oh, how I wanted to know. And, if I don't do anything else, if you stick with me, I will prove to you that I got blindsided by smokestack lightning and it's still teaching me.

While I didn't know it at the time, the shock in that song edged me toward the Saturday morning some years down the road when Coach Chuck Hurd raised the subject that led to my downfall.

Crossroads

I was the first player in his office that Saturday morning. The air smelled like pine cleaner, thank God. There was no tub of chicken livers and hog guts, which he sometimes mixed to nauseate guys with hangovers. It was said the coach could breathe the foulest air without being affected and that the only thing he had a nose for was victory.

I'd gained two hundred yards the night before, a personal best at the time. But the coach could always find something wrong. He criticized my blocking. That ticked me off because I liked to hit and I prided myself on doing my part for other runners, especially my best friend Lee Branch, the fullback who had opened holes for me since middle school. So the coach gave me a grade of "B" for the game. I was Johnny Spink, all-conference tailback, his stud-horse, as he often called me, and he raised the bar for my grade.

But he had trouble being harsh that morning. A strange, dreamy expression came over his face. He looked like a boy fantasizing about a girl. He got up, turned his back to me, and opened the drapes the Booster Club gave him for going 9-2 the season before. It was weird to see drapes instead of stained blinds in a high school coach's office, but these were special, featuring purple bulldogs with spiked collars around their necks and stubble on their snouts. Those drapes were expensive. The Boosters, led by my father, had gone ape with appreciation because Coach Hurd's nine wins last year were the most in school history. Our team, of course, was the Purple Bulldogs. Every school in our conference had a canine of some breed for a nickname, except for the Rebels of lowly Esmeraldo and the Fort Kean Red Raiders, perennial champions.

Coach Hurd looked out at the dew shining on the practice field. "Hear what happened against Esmeraldo last night?" he asked.

"No, sir."

"That kid Dixon for Eagle Forge got him six hundred

yards against the Rebels."

A wad of Red Man bulged in his cheek, and he spat into a wilting paper cup. "Now if Dixon got six hundred, what do you suppose Johnny Spink could get?"

"I don't know, sir."

"How about a thousand?"

I was dumbfounded. A thousand yards was an insane figure. Last year I had gained a hundred and eighty yards in the first quarter against the Rebels. It was the fourth year of their football program, and they hadn't won a game yet. Esmeraldo was a lost place, even by Ozark standards, and the school's high drop-out rate cut the football squad to the bone. Esmeraldo's top football prospects were in the Marines or prison. In the second quarter last fall, I sprained an ankle when I got tangled up with two of my own blockers and had to sit out the rest of the game. Coach Hurd tried to shove me back in there, but Dr. Wardle, our normally milk-blooded team physician, took a stand. I got a grade of "C-" for that game and a dressing-down about learning to play through pain. Although we were winning 60-0, the coach still poured it on at the end. He called a double reverse with six seconds on the clock. It was like Coach Hurd was playing for the NCAA championship.

Michael Gaspeny

He spat again into the sickening paper cup. "Johnny," he said, "no high school back has ever gained a thousand yards in a game. The record right now is 619 yards by Ronney Jenkins in Oxnard, California." He thumped a fat stats book on his desk.

"Why a thousand, Coach?"

"It's a magic number. It grabs attention! You rack up a thousand, and that record's gonna stand a good while. You could be the man, Johnny. You could be the stud. But, son, you need to work on a few things. You're dadgum good when the game's on the line, but you coast when you've got a lead. You got to go like hellfire every play. Life's about kicking butt, Johnny. You get in the habit of lettin' up now, and you'll let up later, I guaran-damn-tee! It's the same on the field and off. They'll eat your lunch if you don't eat theirs first. You got to leave it all between the lines. You can't save nothin' for later. What do you say?"

"All right."

"I can't hear you!"

"Yes-sir!"

"Louder!"

"*Yes-sir!*"

"That's more like it. Send in Lee."

Lee was in the gym, practicing karate blows. He had the

honed look of a dancer rather than the squat build of a fullback. His head was capped with golden curls, and honey-brown hair fit his torso like a vest. He agreed with one of his heroes, Henry David Thoreau, that most clothing was excessive; hence, he liked to go bare-chested in winter and defy the "No shirt-No service" signs in stores. Brutal power lay below his graceful exterior. When he hit you, the nerves went dead and the flesh purpled. As kids, we had been inseparable friends and competitors. He had often left his marks on me.

"You were great last night, Man," I said. "Flying around like a cannonball."

"I'm still flying today," he said. He lowered his voice so the coach couldn't hear him. "Let's drink some beer and smoke some ganja."

"I've got plans."

"Plans to follow Missy's orders."

Coach Hurd summoned Lee, and I went off to join my girlfriend at the car wash where she spearheaded the Pep Club's drive for new band uniforms. On my homemade tape of blues favorites, Albert King bellowed "Angel of Mercy," and I cranked him to the max. For the rest of the afternoon, I wouldn't hear any more blues, so I saturated myself. I hoped to keep the beat in my

Michael Gaspeny

bones because soon I'd be parading down Main Street, waving a sign that urged folks to get their cars washed. Doing chores for Missy wasn't my favorite way to spend a Saturday morning. I was sore from the game last night. It would have been nice to lounge around, listen to my music and read, or drink a Miller High Life forty with Lee. But whatever I did with Lee would disappoint him. I never went far enough for his satisfaction.

It wouldn't take long for me to learn that Coach Chuck Hurd's vision of the thousand-yard game expressed a communal need. Spinkville craved a victory. The town had not benefited from Arkansas' Golden Age. Yes, Bill Clinton was president, the Razorbacks had recently beaten Duke to win the NCAA basketball championship, and there were Wal-Marts and Sam's Clubs outside most American cities in addition to Ozark chicken in most refrigerators. But the same-old, same-old gripped Spinkville. Our only employers of note were the poultry plant, where the jobs were almost hereditary, and Niemann Construction, owned by my girlfriend's father, which did almost all its business outside of town. Otherwise, the major product was obesity or what we call "table muscles," cultivated by the diners, drive-ins, and sweet-shops catering to the local taste for corn dogs, biscuits and white gravy, chili pies, honey buns, and soft-served ice cream sundaes, all fetched pronto by folks who knew you.

As I drove through town to keep my appointment with Missy, everything seemed right in place. But now that I'm looking back at things, it's the jumble I see. Among the eateries on Route 6, there were abandoned homes and scorched-looking trailer parks smack up against churches with landscaped terraces, quaint log-cabin gas stations, and mom-and-pop businesses with pot-holed parking lots and drooping gutters. A nursery school sat next to a junkyard, adjacent to the Tanner Family Funeral Home. To borrow a term from my history book, "rugged individualism" ruled our town, and governmental control was loathed.

But there was one magnetic force of unity, and it wasn't faith or flag. A razorback hog, the insignia for the U. of A's teams, snorted from every building except the houses of God, although some preachers prayed for the Hogs before big games. So many depictions of the pig lined the streets that I could have been driving in a hog stampede. Except for those porkers, everything peeled, faded, or rusted, and many of the signs on the outskirts of town were bullet-riddled.

A Razorback football coach once said northwest Arkansas isn't exactly nowhere, but you can see nowhere from here. The Ozarks are the far west of the South and the far east of the West.

Michael Gaspeny

Sometimes Spinkville seemed more western than southern, because most folks didn't care two twitches of a pig's tail about the family tree. Along with independence and the Razorbacks, we all prized Ozark nights when lights glimmered on the ridges and stars sparkled above the bowl of town. For better and worse, mountain vistas are hypnotic.

Beneath a flagpole bearing a razorback banner, the state flag, and Old Glory, the We The People Laser Wash swarmed with kids snapping cloths, wiping and polishing gleaming machines. A line of drivers awaited service. Missy always raised a crowd. She carried a clipboard and gave instructions. She looked good in her tight, white shorts. We had been together since seventh grade (people often said we might as well be married), and when you've been with a person for five years, you don't always see the particulars. Sometimes she became a bright blur to me. I wondered how anyone could go through a day at a car wash and keep her shorts spotless, but I knew she would.

"Business is jumping," I said.

"It'll jump a lot more with you out front," she answered, giving me a sign and guiding me toward the street.

I paraded, clowning when friends passed and looking serious for adults. It might have been the most beautiful day of the year, the air feeling like mountain lake water, hot on top, but with a cool below that soothed your spine. The soreness from last night's game seemed to ooze out of me and evaporate in the sun. I could have played another game right then. I had one of those moments of wholeness when I felt strong, clean, and grateful for my blessings. I thought I was in charge of my life. I had a fine girlfriend and last night I had gained two hundred yards against a good team, fighting for every blade of grass. It wasn't a bogus achievement like the six hundred yards that Dixon kid had totaled against the Esmeraldo Rebels.

Off in the distance beyond town, autumn quilted the hills in apple and grain shades. I thought of the university up there and how next fall I hoped to carry the ball before the multitudes at Razorback Stadium and at home in front of their TVs. With all the competition, that dream was the longest of long-shots. No Spinkville boy had ever played for the Razorbacks. But there had never been a local boy who could run like me. All I wanted was a chance.

That stretch of sign-bearing in the sun may have been the peak of my high school days. I was thrilled by my life. In my imagination, the sign I held said "Thanks!" and I raised it high above my head.

Michael Gaspeny

Then a big, silver Lincoln carrying two black people rolled by me and into the car wash. You never saw a car like that in town unless it was driven by a poultry king, and you almost never saw a black person in our vicinity unless it was at a gas station on Route 6. It wasn't that Spinkville was segregated. A few blacks had lived here for a short time and moved on. The others were visitors—members of highway work crews staying at the U-Vue Motel or poultry truck drivers sleeping there a night or two. Blacks in Arkansas stayed out of the hills unless they attended the university. Sixty years ago, some Ozark towns had signs saying: "Nigger, don't let the sun set on you in _____!!!" The story of such hospitality passed from one generation of black people to the next.

I knew from my summer study at the university and from my books about the blues that Arkansas had a heart-breaking record of race relations. In the east, when the levees were built along the Mississippi, a mule had more value than a black man. If you worked the animal to death, you got fined and beaten; if you killed a black man, you washed up for dinner. The cotton plantations extended slavery far into the twentieth century. Arkansans mounted such poisonous resistance to the desegregation of schools that President Eisenhower sent federal troops to protect black students integrating Little Rock Central High School.

Racial hatred and violence throughout our history haunted me. After my reading, our savagery was never far from my thoughts. Listening to Big Bill Broonzy, Sonny Boy Williamson, Howlin' Wolf, Robert Nighthawk, and Luther Allison, I thought about the trials these former residents had endured in their home state, which had once marketed itself as "The Land of Opportunity."

The Lincoln with Michigan tags contained a man with skin the tan of a brand-new baseball mitt and a charcoal teenage girl with a wide, self-approving face that seized your eyes and slapped you for looking. In my mind, I put a gardenia in her hair like Billie Holiday had worn. I soon learned that the man and girl were Mr. Charles Futrelle, the new plant manager of Intercontinental Poultry, and his daughter Rae, the soon-to-be genius of the senior class at Spinkville High. Maybe the Futrelles had come to the car wash to measure what the city was like, because the Lincoln didn't look dirty. In fact, during my experience with the Futrelles, everything was maintained at such a high degree of order that you could not have found an unsharpened pencil in their house, and I once heard a minor executive at the plant complain that Mr. Futrelle was such a cleanliness freak that he probably

Michael Gaspeny

polished the change in his pockets.

When the Lincoln took its place in line, it seemed to disturb some of the other machines, which, in my imagination, acquired faces like vehicles in a cartoon. A pick-up truck looked anxious, chuffed, pulled out of line, and slid away. The grille of a station wagon seemed to glare, and the wagon also departed. The Futrelles reached the entrance fast.

Nothing ugly happened. There was no racial incident, but everything became unnatural. As Missy explained the washing options to Mr. Futrelle, she sounded like an actress straining for lines. She looked tense while he drove up on the chocks and the Lincoln was drawn through the laser wash. When the car emerged, the sight of one black man and his daughter turned the kids with chamois cloths into robots. They all did their jobs. The Futrelles' car received the same attention as the vehicles owned by Caucasians. But the day had changed.

Leaving the car wash, Mr. Futrelle turned left toward me. It was my time to redeem the town, my time to recover the fumble. I had the urge to wave. *That's what you'd do for white strangers*, I thought. *That's what you'd do without even thinking*. As the car approached, I felt a tremor in my wrist, but my hand never left my side. Rae gazed beyond me as if I, like the rest of the scene, were beneath her notice. But Mr. Futrelle looked at me, and I must have been a sorry sight. My sign trailed on the pavement. I felt disgusted with myself. Although both Muddy Waters and Howlin' Wolf had been dead for a long time, I had fantasized about the welcome I would have bestowed on my heroes if they had visited Spinkville. Now perhaps I knew. It's always easier to know what's wrong than to do what's right. I guess I had learned something about my role as a pioneer in race relations. There were heavy lessons to come.

Late that afternoon, I paced around the car wash office, feeling sour, while Missy counted the day's proceeds. Her goal had been to collect $700 for band uniforms, and she was pained to be $100 short. Disappointment was built into many of her projects because her ambitions were so high. I never met anyone who expected so much from herself.

"Six hundred dollars is phenomenal," I said. "This town's not bathing in bucks."

"We should have done better. I've got to figure a way to get the rest of the money."

"No one else could have done this well. You did a good job."

"No, I didn't."

That was all the consoling I would do. Her obsessive do-gooding irked me sometimes.

We got into my car, and when I cranked the ignition, my homemade tape of blues favorites screamed at an ear-splitting level. We jumped. I turned the music down and headed toward Burger Boy.

"Who are we listening to?"

"Little Walter Jacobs. 'Key to the Highway.'"

"Oh."

It was her "oh" of dissatisfaction. She liked peppy country music, which I couldn't stand. That bland vanilla sound, like toned-down Lynrd Skynrd with cute lyrics, was pretty much all you heard in Spinkville, except for head-banging metal some kids craved.

"You can turn it off and get some of your music on the radio," I said, but I wasn't sincere.

"No, it's your car."

It was no fun to listen to the blues while she sat there rigidly. I turned the tape off. The radio came on. The band was one of those pressed-jeans, cowboy-hatted Nashville outfits who think they can rock and roll.

She turned the radio off. "I'd rather listen to nothing than music that makes you unhappy. I just don't see why you like that old stuff so much."

That *old* irritated me. "It's only old in years. The sound is brand new, newer than anything out there."

"You're getting that edge in your voice."

She was right. I had a strong desire to give her a lecture about how rock and roll, even in the phony, diluted form she liked, couldn't have existed without the blues.

"Oh, Johnny, let's not fight. It's Saturday night."

She slid across the seat and into the hollow of my arm. I held her as I drove. One of the many things I admired about her was that she showed her needs. Most of the time, I wasn't sure what my needs were, and when I was, I usually hid them. I gave into the occasion, but right then what I really needed was to keep talking until I got to the end of whatever I had to say.

One thing I could not have said was that Rae Futrelle's image had come back to me or that maybe her effect hadn't really left, like an after-image of the sun.

"You know, Johnny," Missy said, "when I took that black man's money, it was the first time I ever touched a black person. I was tense because I was afraid something might go wrong."

Something had gone wrong, I wanted to say: By not

waving, I had done something shameful, but I couldn't open my mouth.

The Lunker

Eight days later, I encountered Mr. F again. Most Sundays, I doled myself out after church—lunch with Missy and her folks; an hour or two with teammates talking trash during the Cowboys' game on TV; then homework, which I liked to do with the falling shadows making a cave of my room. However, that Sunday, shirking obligations, I went fishing. Deep in the woods behind our house, there was a pond on acreage that had been for sale since the time I learned to read the sign. Land was not a hot commodity in Spinkville, which rarely attracted newcomers. Unlike many of the gloomy ponds in my area, ringed by bald banks, full of forlorn stumps, this spot was a bright refuge amid thick sycamore and pine woods, visited by herons and Canada geese.

Michael Gaspeny

I was surprised to see Mr. F dozing there behind a forked stick planted to hold up his rod. Softened by sleep, he looked mild as a boy—the opposite of the dragon portrayed by disgruntled workers at Intercontinental, which had bought the plant from Dad years ago. He wore a camo tee shirt, olive pants, and expensive two-toned insulated boots, light and dark brown. Although he was fifty or so, he had taut muscles and a tough, stubby build. His biceps bulged, veins shaped like forked lightning. By comparison, my father's physique swirled like the Dairy Dream soft-served ice cream treats that became his addiction when he quit drinking. And Coach Chuck Hurd resembled a bloated side of beef.

Mr. F had cast far out into the pond, bottom-fishing for catfish. The tip of his rod quivered, and his line zigzagged through the water.

"Hit!" I yelled. "Hit!"

He lurched to his feet, whipped the rod to set the hook, and played the fish, which hadn't surfaced yet. The line streaked through the water. The panicked fish was running hard. When it slowed to gather energy, Mr. F cranked in a little line, but then the fish burst off again, and Mr. F couldn't make much progress. A fish's fight isn't always equal to its size, but this guy had the power of poundage. I started running. Although Mr. F was strong, his legs teetered as he worked the fish. I thought he might have been drinking, but there were no empties around. Most Spinkville anglers came equipped with a cooler of beer or a pint of Ozark dew, sometimes both as well as tobacco in one form or another.

"Don't horse him!" I yelled from about thirty yards away.

Don't ask me where the expression originated or how horses ever got mixed up with fish. It's what Southerners say in this situation. It calls for being patient and resisting the urge to muscle the fish out of the water because then the line will surely pop. Uncle Roy said it the time I caught my first little sunfish, and I've been saying it ever since. If I had been playing that fish, Mr. F would have said it to me, because, as I soon learned, he came from southern Arkansas.

"That fish has got some heft," I said.

"Or else I've turned to jelly," he answered.

The fish seemed to tire. Mr. F cranked in more and more line until something thick and dark churned the water twenty yards out. I know it's ridiculous, but when the water blackened, I thought of a shark. You don't have to remind me that this pond lay back in the hills six hundred miles from the Gulf of Mexico.

The creature rocketed out of the pond, a blue-black missile of a bass, so breathtaking that Mr. F and I gasped and shouted like seized souls at a revival meeting.

I repeated, "Don't horse him!"

Mr. F looked delirious; in my excitement and envy, I'm sure I did, too. That bass was a once-in-a-lifetime opportunity.

The fish weakened, getting closer and closer to the bank.

"Watch out!" I said. "He might be playing dead."

Sometimes a big fish would go limp and flop on his side, and as soon as you had that boy in the shallows and drew the first breath of victory, it spat out the hook before your aghast eyes. I had lost a couple that way, but never a lunker the size of this fish.

Mr. F said, "Gill him for me. I'm afraid to quit cranking."

"Yes, sir."

He worked the reel behind me as I entered the water, preparing to seize the fish by a gill plate. This apparently simple task carried heavy responsibility. Some of the best fresh-water anglers in America fished all their lives and never saw a bass like this behemoth. Such a trophy catch would grace an angler's memory until the lights went out. But it was also true that the recollection of losing such a beauty would darken many a bright moment. If that lunker slipped from my grip, I would never forgive myself. It would haunt me like a fumble on the goal-line and come between me and Mr. F every time we saw each other. And there was a lot more riding on this moment for me, too, because I had failed to wave at the Futrelles as they left the car-wash. Here I had my chance for minimal redemption. *Please, Lord*, I prayed. *Don't let me lose this fish.*

The bass beat the water around my boots. I bent and scooped with both hands for a gill. As my fingers slid into the bony grooves, the fish stiffened for one last leap, but I clasped him to my chest like a football, slopping from the muck with the bass writhing in my arms. Mr. F worked the hook out of its mouth.

"Get him away from the water," he said, even though the fish was surrounded by grass now.

He pushed the cooler up to the scraggly brush along the woods, flipped the lid, and said, "Stow him."

I packed the fish in there. The bass took up so much room in the small cooler that Mr. Futrelle had to squeeze the top down hard. The lunker crunched in the ice and drummed against the plastic walls.

"How much do you figure he weighs?" Mr. F asked.

"At least twelve pounds."

"Might go thirteen."

I said, "He's the biggest bass I've ever seen. He belongs in a magazine."

"Will you take my picture with him?"

"Sure," I said.

Mr. Futrelle handed me a little camera from his tackle box and hoisted the fish from the cooler.

He was so entranced by his prize that he was almost hugging the fish. "Hold him away from your body," I advised. "Or else his size'll get lost in your shirt."

"Right, right."

I carefully took several pictures, wondering what he was going to do with the fish. Most folks I knew didn't eat bass; no matter how you cooked it or how many lemons you stuck in its mouth, bass tasted like old coins to me. A conservationist wouldn't have stowed the fish. He would have quickly posed for the photograph and tenderly released the lunker. Mr. F had no such sensitivity.

"Look at him!" he marveled, as I opened the cooler. "Hey, boy! Hey, boy!" he said, covering his prey with ice. "You're taking a little trip to the taxidermist. In a month, you'll be mounted on the wall of my office—you will, you will!" That boast would be soon fulfilled.

He pulled his eyes from his mega-prize, and I secured the top of the cooler.

"Thanks for helping me out," Mr. F said, introduced himself, and extended his hand. "You're Johnny Spink. You're all over the papers."

"So are you," I replied as we shook hands. His cost-cutting plans at Intercontinental attracted attention across northwest Arkansas.

He said, "I'm getting that bad boy home right now. Hope to see you down here again soon."

He packed up and headed into the woods, cooler in one hand, rod and tackle box in the other, but he made stumbling progress. He had joy on his face and trouble in his knees. He carried himself like an old soldier. I wondered if his stagger came from a wound in Vietnam. Soon I learned he had acquired an artificial knee from another form of sacrifice.

To stick around and fish would have been anti-climactic. Retrieving my tackle box and heading back into the woods, I realized that while Mr. F and I were working together, I had forgotten our colors. Now that he was gone, my awareness of race returned. I felt happy to have helped a black man—as vain and stupid as that now seems. I had partially compensated for my failure to wave at him outside the car wash. Because I sat in almost constant judgment of myself, I saw life as a gauntlet of challenges to my character. I had passed a small test at the pond. I took my little victory home.

Two days later, when I got up for breakfast before school, Dad flipped me *The Mountain Eagle*, saying, "You're in the news for something other than touchdowns."

My picture of Mr. F and the bass anchored the sports page. He had gotten the big boy weighed by the game warden at Lake Ouachita. At fourteen pounds, one ounce, it awaited certification as a state record for pond-caught bass. The story was written by sports editor Tate Donner, a family friend who had covered my games since Pee Wee Football days. It included Mr. F's account of our landing the bass. Such news was gold in Spinkville where the holy trinity consisted of football, faith, and the fishing report.

When Missy picked me up for school, she said, "So you were fishing while I was waiting for you at church Sunday? I guess you had fun. What's Mr. Futrelle like?"

"Proud. I like the way he carries himself, but he's got shaky legs. He teeters when he walks."

"Was he drinking?"

"No. He might be a veteran."

We stopped at Big Bob's Grab 'N' Go for pre-school colas. Bob was so fat the skin at his throat swung like a bladder when he moved. He asked, "Was the bass really that big?"

"A fresh-water Jaws," I said.

"Damn, I been fishing back there for years!"

"Tell me about it!" I said.

That night, Mr. F called and invited me and Dad to dinner Sunday evening. Dad would be out of town, but I accepted.

Mr. F said, "At the plant today, everybody wanted to talk fishing. They were more productive. They're also talking up the Purple Dogs going undefeated this year."

I avoided thoughts of a perfect season, concentrating on one opponent at a time, but Coach Chuck Hurd's craving for a thousand-yard game often cut into my thoughts.

I was excited about dinner with Mr. F and Rae, who had hypnotic curves and a stratospheric mind that immediately made her the star of our World Lit class. This would be my first meal with black people, and I did not want to embarrass myself. I asked Dad for advice.

"Be your self," he said. "People always like you. Black people are just like white people."

That sounded reassuring at first, but I would come to have my doubts.

That Friday, we had a home game against the Mount Ida

Mastiffs. After school, I went home to lie around and listen to music. Dad always fixed me a steak and baked potato—not too much, not too little—served three hours before I took the field.

I sorted through the mail which consisted of the usual recruiting letters from small colleges and two-year schools. I longed for a letter decorated with a snorting Razorback, but no NCAA-Division I institution had shown an interest in me because I played way back in the hills against weak competition. If I never heard from Fayetteville, I was determined to be a walk-on.

The game against Mount Ida, billed as a test against a tough team, had a dream-like ease. The Mastiffs' defensive linemen were big as hogs and just as slow. Lee's blocks laid them out, and I flashed through the holes Lee blasted open. I gained three hundred yards, my new personal best, but it seemed like a gift I hadn't earned. Something Ms. Colwin said in World Lit worried me: "Whom the gods would destroy, they first indulge." We had been reading excerpts from *The Odyssey,* and I felt as if Athena and Hermes had glided me through the game. I wasn't tired; I had no aches; I felt like I'd coasted. When Tate Donner appeared with pad and pen, I said, "The most valuable player in this game was Lee Branch. He was a blocking beast. I just collected the yards Lee gave me." On the way to the locker room, I was dazed by my luck. Mr. F broke my trance, shook my hand, and congratulated me. It was the first game he'd seen, and I felt proud to have done well in front of him.

"Bring a good appetite Sunday night," he said.

In the morning, while Coach Chuck Hurd berated me for failing to give one hundred and ten percent, I thought about Rae more than any guy with a steady girl had a right to do. Rae was "built up from the ground," as so many blues songs said in appreciation of a spell-casting, natural woman. I was afraid to look at her too long. Girls always sensed when that was going on. I did not want to spend the dinner blushing.

What would I say to her? Missy and I had always been the best students in AP courses, but Rae left us in the dust. She and Ms. Colwin seemed like two experts discoursing while the rest of us squirmed. I liked Rae's clear, confident Midwestern tone so much that even when I had a comment, I let her go first. I did not want to miss a syllable. Some kids called her a "Know-It-All," which was accurate because she did know it all and she didn't restrain herself.

During dinner that Sunday, while Mr. F and I dug into steaks he had expertly grilled and plenty of side dishes, Rae ate something leafy. I started off badly with her by mentioning how

Michael Gaspeny

much I loved the blues. I had the dumb notion that a black girl would be more sympathetic to my tastes than my friends were.

"That old-timey stuff? It's depressing," she said, sounding like Missy.

I wanted to say that plenty of blues songs were funny, but I knew it would be a lost cause. So I asked, "What do you listen to?"

"Inspirational music—classical and gospel. I like to have positive thoughts, and that's not easy around here."

Mr. F interrupted. "Johnny's folks settled this town. His father's a progressive mayor."

I felt Rae biting her tongue and heard what she held back—"Progress? Then why is this town so dead?" I was torn between agreeing with her and defending my father.

I changed the subject. "Don't you think Ms. Colwin's a great teacher?"

"She's wonderful. Ms. Colwin and my music keep me going."

Rae couldn't open her mouth without expressing her superiority. I wanted to ask why she didn't go back to the Motor City. Sometime later Mr. F told me Rae and her mother didn't get along.

She deigned to clear the table. To escape the temptation of watching her move, I helped, but all of her entranced me. Rae's beautiful lips curved like little bows. Below her cheekbones, the long, concave sides of her face glowed like oiled walnut. I imagined my fingers slowly tracing her profile. In the kitchen, I was sure she read my thoughts.

Mr. F called from the dining room. "Did you know Coach Hurd dropped by the plant last week? He's got folks buzzing about the thousand-yard game."

I blurted, "No! He's shameless."

"Then he was born to be a football coach."

I looked for the effect of our talk on Rae, but she was gone, leaving two pieces of pecan pie on plates. Classical music rose from the back of the house. It wasn't "Moonlight Sonata," the extent of my knowledge in that field.

After we ate the pie, I waited a few polite, digestive minutes, thanked my host, and said, "I better get going."

"What a minute! You and Rae were talking about the blues. I just remembered something. When I was a kid, I met Muddy Waters."

"What? He's one of my idols!"

Memory widened his eyes. He said, "It was springtime

in Drumlin, where I grew up. I was six or seven. My Daddy and I were fishing at a pond, catching these big, plump shellcrackers spawning in the weeds along the bank. There was a juke joint back in the pines not far from there. A bronze Cadillac came rolling down the sand road from the juke. The driver saw our Croker sacks stuffed with fish. He stopped and said, 'Gentlemen, Muddy Waters is at Ermaline's, and he's talking about a fish-fry. I know he'd buy these fish from you. I'd give you a ride back there, but I don't want no fish smell in the car. Muddy's particular about his vehicle.'

"Now Daddy never went to a juke joint, but that morning he must have felt bold. You know how catching a mess of fish can give you some zip. So we cleaned out that shellcracker nest and walked a ways up to Ermaline's, which wasn't much more than a big shack. I just about jumped at the commotion coming out of that place. The juke box was pounding, and the hollering sounded like thunderclaps. I trailed inside behind Daddy. There were five men playing poker and yelling. They wore wilted tuxedos from performing in Little Rock or Memphis the night before. In front of each man was a pistol, a pint of whiskey, and a stack of bills. When my Dad saw the guns, the spunk went out of him.

"Muddy Waters stood up, welcomed us in this big, warm

voice, and was gracious as could be. He was broad-shouldered with processed hair and heavy-lidded eyes that looked a little Indian. He offered Daddy whiskey and me a Coke, but Daddy had stiffened up. He made an excuse about us having to get back home. As pleasant as Muddy Waters was, he was used to living with guns, and I guess it didn't occur to him that pistols would bother somebody else, especially folks out in the sticks. Daddy sold the fish, and we got out of there. On the way home, Daddy kept shaking his head and saying, 'I never should have taken you in that place. Don't you say a word to your mother.' At home, he said to her, 'Fish just weren't biting today, but look what we found. A twenty dollar bill came blowing down the road. And we want you to have it.'

"I don't mean to say Muddy Waters was a bad man. In fact, the opposite was true. He had a big heart and never forgot the people down home in what they used to call 'the old country.' But, see, Johnny, those guys came up the hard way, picking cotton and plowing fields instead of going to school—running off, hopping boxcars, sleeping on pool tables, and God knows what else. A kid on the road is easy pickings, if he's not lucky. I know those guns were mostly for show. But it says a lot about where you come from and how you live if you represent yourself that way.

Michael Gaspeny

They grew up rough. Their music wouldn't have such a dangerous sound if they hadn't been up against it."

That was the first time Mr. F had told me something he thought I should know. From there, it would happen every now and then. When my father instructed me, I drifted away. That night my mind began taping most everything Mr. F had to say, and I'm still playing those tapes.

I rose from the table and thanked him for everything.

"Thank *you*," he replied. "I should put you on the payroll. You're building unity at the plant. You take folks' minds off me."

We shook hands at the door. Rae didn't tear herself from her music to bid me a fond farewell. Trotting down the hillside to my car, I yearned to be in her room.

In the morning, Missy and I were talking before World Lit when Rae handed me my polarized sunglasses, saying, "Daddy asked me to return these after *he* had you over for dinner."

Throughout class, Missy shifted around in her desk. Once the bell rang and we were in the hall, she said, "I thought you worked on your Latin translation last night. You had dinner with her and you didn't tell me?"

"Listen: Rae was at the table, but I had dinner with Mr.

Futrelle. He invited me for helping him catch his bass. You know the story. To tell you the truth, Rae wasn't happy to see me."

"I don't like it when you keep things from me, Johnny," she said.

I should have broken up with her right then, not because of her jealousy, but because of my crush on Rae.

Often, after that, Missy asked prying questions such as "What's it like at the Futrelles?"

"Pleasant. Mr. Futrelle has the same recliner as your dad."

One night she said, "I think Rae likes you." She was only fishing.

"Likes me? She doesn't even like to look in my direction. She thinks me and my family are responsible for the low state of culture in Spinkville. Rae doesn't like anybody here but Ms. Colwin."

I wasn't lying. Rae had never shown one glimmer of interest in me or my conversation. The attraction was all mine. However, my forceful denial increased Missy's suspicion.

It was a month before I would take the field against Esmeraldo, and my thoughts flip-flopped about the record. In the beginning, the thousand-yard game seemed like a scheme to glorify Coach Chuck Hurd and grab cheap renown for me and the

Purple Dogs. But it had swelled into a campaign for civic pride. In the Mockingbird Café, across from the courthouse, a town commissioner floated the idea of a sign at the city limits to commemorate my upcoming feat. Some bigwigs considered the record a sure thing. The Chamber of Commerce was panting to brighten Spinkville's dreary image. When Bill Clinton, "The Man from Hope," reached the White House, business boomed in our state, but his rise didn't raise Spinkville. In northwest Arkansas, retirement communities flourished in Rogers and Bentonville; anglers flocked to Ozark marinas, spurred by TV fishing-show hosts like Bill Dance and Roland Martin; evangelical Christians on tour buses prayed at the Christ of the Ozarks, stayed at chalet-like hotels in Eureka Springs, and relished family pursuits in Harrison. Not so far away from us, Branson, Missouri had become the new mecca of country music and clean fun.

Folks without a profit motive wanted the record, too, because they fanatically identified with the fortunes of the Purple Dogs, their team. They craved bragging rights rising from a spotless, undefeated season and a national rushing record to exalt. Who was I to deny such pleasure? And, of course, I had my own claim to stake. Glorious headlines might help my case with the Razorback recruiters avoiding me now.

Doubt and tension increased the power of the blues and football in my life. Cruising around town, I played tapes at ear-splitting levels, shouting the lyrics, pounding the steering wheel, and feeling superior to the lower species addicted to sappy Nashville tunes. I heard the blues in my head as I pushed myself and my teammates hard in practice. I pumped through every drill and reveled in the grunts and grime. Coach Chuck Hurd's favor shone upon me.

One Saturday Dad and I made our annual football trip to Fayetteville to watch the Hogs gore the competition. In the old days, we never missed a home game, but now this was the only traveling we did. I hadn't been many places. All I could remember of the trips we made with my mother to New Orleans and Chicago were the fights that broke out because she didn't want to go home. A few years back, the one big trip Dad and I took had flopped—a June visit to Uncle Roy in the Keys. The vacation was hard on my father, who has no tolerance for the outdoors. Despite precautions, the mosquitoes tore into him, and the sun blistered the tops of his feet. Roy took us sight-casting for bonefish, but Dad couldn't get the hang of it, and he kept apologizing, which made matters worse. His casts landed behind the fish, and he embarrassed him-self by hooking the tail of a sleeping nurse shark. I had better

Michael Gaspeny

timing and caught a few bonefish, which Roy released. Behind a chipper façade, Dad was pained by the glaring environment, and he was anxious for the tormenting trip to end. It's always been hard for me to tolerate weakness, and I thought badly of him. As unfair as it was, I compared Dad's marshmallow physique with Roy's wide muscularity. I hoped I would never look like my father.

Football addiction had always been our bond. I never felt so close to him as I did on those Saturday pilgrimages to call the Hogs in Fayetteville and Sundays when we shared our mania for the Cowboys. Returning to Fayetteville and his university was therapy for Dad, who was heavily involved in the alumni organization. He seemed to know everyone. He entered the stadium pressing flesh and paying special attention to the afflicted and the old. He decorated himself in the insignia of the Boar, from hog helmet to necktie to porkers snorting flames on his socks. He placed the helmet over his heart as he sang the alma mater.

It entertained me to see Dad unwind. The U. of A., where he had distinguished himself, was holy to him. Once he took me to the law school library and showed me the oak table where he had studied for years. I thought he might kneel and offer a prayer of gratitude. I hoped to find such a sacred place in my life. My shrine would be Razorback Stadium itself, where I wanted one day to bring my own son to visit the site of my heroics.

That particular Saturday had been ordered from the catalog of grace. In the brilliant, cloudless sweater-weather, a faint silver moon arced over the grain-shaded valley beyond the stadium, while the Hogs bashed TCU. Afterward, I still felt the sun on my face as Dad and I feasted at Herman's Ribhouse. Dusk deepened as we left the restaurant and began the descent home. The day had been a great escape, but as we rode the switchbacks along highway 71 to Spinkville, my problems jumped me.

"I sure would like to score some touchdowns up there," I said. "But it won't be easy. Most of their running backs come from Dallas or LA."

"God makes the same legs in Spinkville as he does in Los Angeles," Dad replied. "Don't be intimidated."

"I wish I could play against stronger competition."

"You can't pick your opponents. You have to take what you're given."

"I wish Esmeraldo wasn't a part of it," I said.

I wanted an ally, and my father was known for his compassion.

"Are people pressuring you?"

"Yeah, but that's not the worst part. See, I don't know if I want the record."

The car swerved, nosing out over the double yellow line for an instant, tires squealing. Dad slowed down and eased us back on our side of the road.

"Why don't you want the record?"

"It's too easy. Esmeraldo's been a doormat since I can remember. They're a small school so far back in the hills they don't have many players to choose from. Nobody ends up there, even by accident. A lot of their guys drop out of school and get into trouble."

"That's no excuse to let up on them. When a team lines up for the kick-off, it takes its chances."

"But the record's not worth anything."

"Maybe not to you."

This was not the talk I was hoping to have. "But, Dad," I said. "You've always taught me to make up my own mind and not be swayed by the crowd."

"That's true, Johnny, but sometimes you have to carry the ball for others."

"Even if what they want is wrong?"

"I don't think it's wrong to want to feel community pride.

The people here made us rich. When we can give something back, I think we ought to."

I'd had enough. Turning on my Walkman, I filled my ears with Robert Johnson. When we reached Spinkville, Dad resumed his appeal, but the only line I heard was "You've given people so much to look forward to."

It was Coach Chuck Hurd who had given folks so much to look forward to. At the head of that crowd stood my father. Dad was no rebel; he believed in the old system of achievement and reward. One side of his study was decorated with the honors he had won, the other with framed newspaper stories describing my pigskin heroics. I completed him.

After that trip to the mountains, I felt bad about myself. Dad's hypocrisy was minor in comparison to mine. He strove constantly for what he loved—his university, town, and me. So what if he prized recognition? How honest was I, going through the motions with Missy while craving Rae? Mr. F was my friend, and I dreamed of taking his daughter's clothes off.

Although it was a bye week for the Spinkville Purple Dogs, Coach Chuck drove us through merciless practices, even on Saturday, so I did not feel like putting on itchy clothes and going to church Sunday. My guilt about leaving Missy and her parents in the pew by themselves did not outweigh my desire to fish. When I reached the pond with rod and tackle box, five anglers, seeking their own lunkers, had already staked out spots in what had become the town honey-hole. They made the refuge look a lot smaller, and they would keep the herons away. Then Mr. F came teetering down the hill at the other end of the pond. We waved to the others watching their lines in the water as they ate honey buns and slurped coffee from thermoses. By noon, they'd be popping beers.

Mr. Futrelle and I put our heads together and decided to go to Lake Ouachita, where he bought bait and ice from a ranger, drawing a bill from a gold clip. Its glint and wedge of green caught many an eye that fall. We took cups of bloodworms and a bucket of minnows to a clearing we liked and fished for crappie. It was prime season for those flashing, silver-blue beauties that fried up crisp and tasted sweet. They are what anglers call "an eating fish."

The crappie were running. By mid-morning, the cooler was full of fish scraping in the ice. The sun came on. The bites stopped. Our carrot bobbers drifted on the lake. We took it easy. I asked about the plant.

"Production's picking up. But there are still some folk

used to being useless. I guess that's why your daddy sold out."

"He didn't really like business. He wanted to help people."

"He was like that at the university. There was a lot of trouble between students and the administration when I was up there. He was SGA president. Both sides trusted him."

"So you went to school up there?"

"In a manner of speaking. Yep, in Fayetteville, that's where I got my education."

I would come to prize the story he started that day as much as my music and books.

"Ever been to Drumlin?" he asked.

"No. All I know is it's down south in Arkansas, not far from Louisiana."

"Mostly swamp and a paper mill. I played a lot of football down there, but I wasn't going anywhere. I didn't have your speed. I was a plugger. I could hit and take a lick. That was about it."

He was talking my language. Out over the lake, I saw him churning into tacklers.

"I loved to play, but it looked like I'd follow my daddy's footsteps into the lumber mill. Then one night a man in a red blazer came to our door, carrying a briefcase. We lived on the edge of town. No white person had ever been to our house. Through the screen, he told me his name, Jack DeRoza, and asked to speak to my father."

Mr. F shook his head and repeated the stranger's name. "He was a Razorback when I was a little kid. He wasn't a legend or even close, but when the kids played football with one of those little pigskins from a gas station give-away, we borrowed names from the games on the radio, and somebody always said, 'I'm Jack DeRoza.'

"My head zoomed. Daddy came to the door and said, 'Sorry, but I've got all the insurance we need.' Jack said, 'How about a free policy for your son Charley's future? But it comes with one hard obligation. Sir, I hope you'll hear me out.'

"I think the word 'hard' got him in the house. Johnny, my heart was pumping. I wondered if a Razorback coach had seen something about me that even I didn't know. Maybe they wanted me to block. What Jack offered was a full-ride for four years for me to be on the scout team. 'What kind of team?' Daddy asked. 'Boy Scout team?'

"Jack explained that scouts ran opponents' offenses in practice so that the team could prepare for upcoming games. He said, 'We need strong, tough guys like Charley to tote the ball against our defense.'

'You mean to be tackling dummies?' Daddy asked.

'At the university, we like to think of the scouts as sparring partners, Mr. Futrelle.'

'That's a dirty deal!'

'Yes, sir, one side of a scout-teamer's life is mud and pain. But the other side opens on a bright future. The university's the hope of our state. It's where kids find themselves and make connections. We can give Charley the best Arkansas has to offer.'

"Daddy said, 'No kind of father would send his son to be cannon fodder. We appreciate you stopping by.'

"Jack DeRoza picked up his briefcase, thanked us for listening, said he'd be at the Midway Motel till eleven the next morning, and left.

"Daddy was known for his even temper, but, Johnny, that day he exploded in a floor-shaking tirade. 'What do you suppose the color of that scout team is? If there's a white scout, *I'll* pay for his scholarship. Scout team, rout team! Black boys getting crippled so white coaches can win!'

"Johnny, I'd never thought much about the world beyond Drumlin, but Jack DeRoza woke me up. I said, 'Some of us are

Michael Gaspeny

playing up there now, Daddy. Times are changing. What am I going to do if I stay here?'

'Have pride,' he answered.

'At the mill?' I said.

'Better this mill than their mill. What kind of pride is there in getting your butt kicked? You don't know what's in store for you up there.'

'That's why I have to go,' I said."

Mr. Futrelle's bobber darted. He jerked himself up, staggered, and would have toppled if I hadn't caught him.

I regretted the interruption, because he'd taken me somewhere I was glad to go.

The Knight in Their Midst

My life in Spinkville was never the same after Ms. Colwin explained the concept of *noblesse oblige* in World Lit one morning toward the end of October. She might as well have rung the bell in the courthouse square to announce that I no longer belonged to myself.

She linked the definition to a work from the medieval period. The teacher herself was a long way from the Middle Ages. The statuesque Ms. Colwin had a long ribcage, the hollow belly of a distance runner, and tapered legs. Her figure made her *hot* to us guys. Before football practice, boys banged on their lockers and bellowed savage pleas for some personal time with the teacher. I wanted her, too, but I'd noticed that my desire burned at a lower

Michael Gaspeny

temperature than other guys'. There seemed to be more dog in them than there was in me, and sometimes I questioned my manhood. Heat was a secondary matter in my relationship with Missy. My desire for other girls was only urgent now and then, until Rae came to town. I had never wanted a girl like I did her.

"*Noblesse oblige*," Ms. Colwin explained, "literally means 'nobility obliges.' It was what a nobleman owed his subjects for their allegiance." Gliding down an aisle of desks, she continued, "It was an ideal, rather than something written on parchment, an assurance that the aristocrat would perform acts of generosity and charity. It promised that he would step down from his high place and fulfill the needs of the people from time to time.

"Imagine there was football in those days," she said, my ears suddenly rising. "And the people yearned for the count to lead a great victory over a neighboring estate. Then he would have to honor that desire in order to maintain the homage of his people. He would venture forth like a certain *knight in our midst* to set records for his subjects."

Her attempt at wit infuriated me. The students laughed as they always did when dull history was enlivened by a local connection, and they looked at me with approval. Missy sat behind me, so I couldn't show her my resentment. When I glanced at Rae, hoping for understanding, she looked disgusted. I wanted to leap up and denounce the record, but I was too mad to make sense, and my rant would have hurt many of my classmates. They had an optimistic outlook I did not want to disrupt. Nor did I wish to explode in front of Rae.

When the bell rang, I went straight to my car—a violation of school policy with a penalty of a month of Saturday mornings in detention. I jammed in my tape of Delta Bluesmasters and listened repeatedly to Robert Nighthawk's shrieking slide guitar on "Goin' Down to Eli's." I cranked the volume up to a deranged level and screamed along with Robert: "Gonna murder my baby / If she don't stop cheatin' and lyin'." I wasn't raving about a woman. I wanted to kill my roots. Sick of my status as an aristocrat and a knight, I wanted to be a twelve-year-old bluesboy hopping freights.

When I got out of the car, music dinning in my head, I saw a ninth-grader heading to his mom's rusted Chevy for a doctor's appointment. On his Dallas Cowboys' sweatshirt, he wore a football-shaped badge identifying him as a member of the "Grab a Grand Club." It was illustrated by a ball carrier with 11 on his jersey, my number, soaring over a hurdle in the form of 1000. He told me the Booster Club sold the badges for $3 apiece. He probably got $5 allowance a week, if he was lucky, and he had shot sixty percent on me. He had no idea how shaky his investment was or what an emblem of disappointment the badge might become. When I reentered the school, the hall monitor saluted me. I was beyond the law.

As the idiotic badges multiplied around me, I retreated farther into music and fantasies about Rae. I imagined she possessed the power to make me feel more alive than the combined electricity of every touchdown I had ever made. If only I had the key. Such thoughts fed one side of my nature and nauseated the other. How much of my burning was natural and how much was as tyrannical as a slave master's lust? Was there any way to separate myself from the crimes of my race?

After practice one day, I went to Lee Branch's to let off steam. He had lived in the garage of his adoptive parents' ranch house since he was fourteen. He called his domain "Lee's Golden Lounge." His easy-going folks, semi-retired on army pensions, sold produce and flowers at the square on Saturdays and ran a stall at the flea market. They had held desk jobs at Fort Bragg, North Carolina, where Lee lived until he was eleven. There, spell-bound by sky-diving shows, he acquired his ambition to be a paratrooper.

Lee pursued self-discipline and self-destruction almost

equally. The garage contained a heavy bag to absorb his karate blows; his old scratchy Doors and Led Zeppelin records, which he considered more authentic than tapes and CD's; enough Beat and Buddhist literature to open a reading room; a refrigerator loaded with beer, fruit, and vegetables; and a bong. He craved "babes" with big breasts, and most of the well-endowed girls in our area had been entertained at the lounge.

I parked in front of the garage and tried to get Lee's attention. Coach Chuck Hurd had put us through a vicious practice, but nothing fazed Lee. He was perfecting karate kicks at the center of a Led Zep storm. The song was "You Need Love."

I banged on the garage door until he finally let me in. Turning down the record player, I couldn't resist mocking his music.

"'You Need Love,' written by Willie Dixon, performed by McKinley Morganfield, a.k.a. the incomparable Muddy Waters, released by Chess Records, 1963. Why get the watered-down taste?"

"Who cares who wrote it? Led Zep roars. You're too historical. Let's drink some beer!"

"We've got a game tomorrow night."

"Then let's get loaded. It'll give us hangovers, and that'll make us horny, and we'll hit like beasts during the game, and then I'm taking Luella Lang to the mat all night long."

"OK, I'll have a 40."

"Damn right!"

On the drain board next to the sink stood a half-gone Miller 40. Lee had gotten busy as soon as he reached home from Coach Chuck's two-on-one drills. I wanted to see another side of me. Lee lived by binges of vice and purification. When he drank, he could swing from charming to mean. I sat on the mat covering most of the garage and propped my back against the wall.

Night fell. Lee replaced Led Zep with a beautiful record blending John Coltrane's captivating sax and Johnny Hartman's cosmopolitan voice on standards like "They Say It's Wonderful" and "My One and Only Love." Lee had great taste in jazz. The music made Manhattan shimmer outside the lounge. I imagined me and Rae dancing close in a cozy night spot, even though I couldn't dance worth a damn.

Lee said, "As soon as I saw those badges, I knew you'd be dropping in."

"They make me sick."

"I'm going to buy one and put a big black slash mark through it."

"Do it!" I said.

I told him about Ms. Colwin's class and Rae's pained look. The presence of a friend and the wistful music opened me. I talked about Rae.

"Call her."

"What?"

"Call her now."

"She doesn't want to hear from me."

"How do you know? Here." He put the rotary phone at my feet.

"What if Mr. Futrelle answers? He's a friend of mine."

"Tell him 'Good evening' and ask to speak to Rae. Then ask her to come over here and hang out with us."

"In the garage?"

I didn't think she'd find the lounge inspiring, especially with Robert Plant screaming about how girls needed cooling and Jim Morrison singing "Crawling King Snake," a John Lee Hooker cover. I wondered if Lee would put on a shirt.

He said, "We could ask her to do weird things like have a conversation and eat some pizza. I'll bet she's got some interesting ideas. Call her. All she can say is 'no.'"

"What would Missy think?"

"In the first place, she wouldn't have to know. In the second place, would you rather spend some time with Rae or be on your old lady's leash? What are you afraid of?"

"Me."

"Precisely."

I watched his Adam's apple bob as he glugged beer. He sighed with pleasure. He savored analyzing my problems. He switched from friend to guru.

"The whole time I've known you, the only two things you ever got excited about are football and the blues. You've been living kind of an arranged life. Your days are like clothes waiting for you in the closet, and you get up and put them on." Lee paused to admire his comparison. The bastard loved his expert's tone. "Now then, Rae moves you, but you don't do a thing about it. Scenario: It's thirty years down the road. My folks have died. I come back here to put the house on the market. You and me are in the garage, having a few misty brews, and you say, 'Gee, remember Rae? I wonder what would've happened if I'd called her that night you gave me the phone.'"

I had come there to relax, and this is what I got.

I said, "Doctor, are you going to bill me for this session?"

"The senseis always say, 'Get yourself out.'"

"What's that supposed to mean?"

"You make the call."

"I'm going," I said, left Lee's Golden Lounge, and drove off in a red fog of resentment.

When we were younger, our disagreements were piddling, quickly-mended tiffs, but now, more and more, Lee liked to hurt me with his honesty. It had become the price of ducking into the lounge. I wanted to retaliate, but he didn't have any weaknesses. He was strong, handsome, well-read, successful with girls (and a few older women). Self-reliant, he lived as he pleased. He attended school regularly only during football season, but the principal never questioned his absences. The whole town was afraid to challenge Lee Branch.

From my tape player Bo Diddley demanded "Who Do You Love?" The subject closed in on me. I hated Lee's God imitation, but he was right: I had to do something. I mulled over his mumbo-jumbo. What did he mean by "Get yourself out?" Escape from my routine, leave town? Or had he said, "Get your *self* out"? Was that a challenge to show my real self? But I didn't really know anymore what my real self was.

The next night we faced Fort Kean, perennial conference champs. We hadn't beaten the Red Raiders in eleven years, since I

Michael Gaspeny

was seven years old. I didn't remember that game, but, according to Dad, I was there. I had either attended or played in one hundred and seven Spinkville High games, at least seventy of which were defeats.

Fort Kean, located in the foothills sixty miles below us, was known for its orchards. It was the only place in our corner of the state with an appreciable black population, maybe ten percent. Early in the century, blacks had been recruited to pick fruit, and some had stayed. Half the Red Raiders were black, and that gave me extra incentive because sportswriters in the mountains, including Tate Donner, often said, though not in print, that our teams choked against black competition.

No matter how hard I struggled, I couldn't get unwound against Fort Kean. Its coach, Ronnie Mallard, knew Chuck Hurd hated to pass, so he dared us to throw the ball, shooting linebackers into the gaps and sometimes piling eight men on the line, overwhelming my blockers. Coach Chuck didn't adjust his Stone Age game plan. The Red Raiders jammed Lee in the backfield. Tacklers formed thickets around me almost as soon as I got the ball. I averaged a measly two yards a carry in the first half, and I almost maimed myself to get that. But our defense played well, and we went to the locker room at the half down 6-0, in contrast to the slaughters Fort Kean normally inflicted on us.

Another coach would have changed tactics, but that wasn't Coach Chuck's style. He urged us to hit harder and told me I was too slow finding the hole, even though in the swarm around me, I hadn't seen a sliver of light. I had done nothing to attract the attention of university recruiters there to evaluate the prime prospects on the Red Raiders.

But midway through the fourth quarter, the score unchanged, we tried a delay up the middle from our own 15. Lee toppled a blitzing linebacker, and I leapt a tackler at the line of scrimmage, cut sharply to my left, eluding an airborne cornerback, and as I flew upfield, there was no one near me for thirty yards. I would like to say that I was mindless as a flashing colt, but all that space provided too much freedom to think. The possibilities for humiliation rose in my head—first, a fumble as I shifted the ball to my outside arm, but I realized I'd already made the transfer; second, a fumble when I was hit; third, tripping over my own feet; fourth, mincing out of bounds when the next tackler drew an angle on me.

I sensed someone behind me. I veered toward midfield, feeling that tackler skidding on his gut where I had been. Now I raced at two Red Raiders who seemed to have risen from the ground, zapping my time to ponder. I struck the first with a stiff-arm, quicker and harder than I had ever cracked anyone in all my life. I crushed him. The thrill of the blow shot through me from palm to sole and made me delirious. Then the second guy jumped me from behind and twisted my neck. I carried him for about five yards, and he would've wrenched me down, but I braked and bucked my back. He flew off me like a shell, and I bolted into the end zone and looked back for a flag. When the referee's arms shot upright, I raced in crazy circles. The ref beckoned for the ball. I knew I was in danger of drawing a penalty for unsportsmanlike conduct, so I tucked the ball in his arms. Johnny James's extra point split the uprights, and we beat Fort Kean, 7-6. Dad danced on the field, floating the Spinkville pennant. I believe it was one of the sweetest moments in his life. It may have been the only time since I became a teen that he and I were released simultaneously from the pressure of our minds.

Missy hugged me as we passed through the crowd slapping my pads. I shouted and traded high-fives. Dad threw an arm over my shoulder, and I walked between him and Missy. Mr. F, waiting among the fans outside the locker room, edged forward to congratulate me. I was surprised to see Rae off to the side, her distance and aloof eyes emphasizing that she'd been dragged along. It was embarrassing to receive Mr. F's praise, because I never wanted to be the center of attention when he was around. I introduced him to Missy, who was gracious, mentioning how many good things I had said about him. I felt a surge of warmth toward her. Rae didn't come forward, so I approached her.

"I didn't know you were a football fan," I said.

"I'm not, of course. But Dad wanted to be here. 'When in Rome,' I suppose. I am glad you won," she conceded in her perfectly clear Midwestern voice.

Off to the side, I noticed Lee watching. I couldn't imagine anyone appearing more heroic, with his tangled gold curls, intense gaze, and Luella Lang, his playmate of the month, looped around his waist. But he wasn't enjoying himself, and I wondered if my analyst had noticed some new failing of mine.

Then the celebration swept me away from the Futrelles and Lee's appraisal. I kept hearing Rae's haughty *When in Rome*. No matter. It thrilled me to think she had seen the best run of my life and the joy it generated. That had to make an impression on her.

When Missy, Dad, and I got home, *Prep Pigskin High-lights* opened with a teaser from my touchdown. Later, the run was shown in full, with Coach Chuck Hurd commenting as if he himself had carried the ball.

Next morning, in *The Mountain Eagle*, Tate Donner's coverage of the game bore the headline "Fabled Run Vaults Spinkville over Fort Kean." Sidebars explored the long drought against the Red Raiders and the possibility of an unbeaten season.

When I reached the coach's office for our Saturday meeting, I said, "I saw you on TV last night, Coach."

A shy look crossed his fierce face. "Thank you," he replied. It was such a ridiculous statement that it made me like him for the moment. He, too, had no idea how to handle celebrity, even our little brush with it.

"Now, son," he said and spat Red Man juice into a two-liter cola bottle and began critiquing my performance, which was not altogether acceptable in his eyes. Despite the fabled dash that put him on TV, I had missed a few blocks and sometimes failed to grind until the whistle.

Construction sounds interrupted him. He spat, rose, opened his Purple Dog drapes, and looked across the practice field to the stadium.

"What's going on?" I asked.

"They're building a new press box, Johnny. That old four-seater is a thing of the past."

Yes, the old press box had resembled a shabbily-built tree house reached by a rickety ladder. It rocked in a high wind. The few reporters covering our games chose the stands.

"You wouldn't believe the interest in the Esmeraldo game," the coach continued. "We're getting requests for press credentials. Us, a Class-D school in the crickets! The Booster Club is going to set up a hospitality room inside the school. *Sports Illustrated* called me for background information."

"Do you think The Pope will come?" I joked.

For an instant, he truly seemed to consider accommodating the pontiff. Then he laughed and said, "You're getting cheeky, son. You're a shoo-in for Class Wit."

Throughout this meeting, the power had shifted. I had the heady sensation that I could lead him around like a pony.

"Tell me, Coach, what's in the record for you?"

"I'm a flat-lander, Johnny. I'd like to go home to a Class-B school with a solid tradition. You take enough foggy bus rides on slick mountain roads, and it's only so long before you end up in the ditch, if there is one. Besides, the coach's name goes in that record book, too. Now let's talk about how to get us there."

We had games against Chinquapin and Squaw Hollow before Esmeraldo. The coach discussed inserting a few new plays.

Michael Gaspeny

Then the construction noise grew to such a roar that we had to go the gym to finish our parley.

That Sunday afternoon, Mr. F and I watched the Cowboys game on the big TV in his den. We spent time together every Sunday except for the weekend each month when he flew to Michigan to visit his wife, president of the Detroit chapter of the NAACP.

Our attention drifted from the Cowboys clobbering the Falcons. Neither of us enjoyed a slaughter.

"Did you serve in Vietnam?" I asked.

"No, no," he answered. "After I paid my dues on the scout team, I was 4-F."

I thought about how many blues songs involved paying your dues.

Feeling my interest, he asked, "Johnny, have you ever played for a terrible football team getting a butt-whipping every game?"

"I've been on losers, but we always won a few games."

"On the scout team, we didn't play games. There wasn't a score to keep. We were hired hands running plays and getting whipped. Football wasn't fun anymore. Back in high school, people respected us because we were on the team, but now there was nothing for people to respect or us to be proud of. We didn't even travel with the team. At home games, we walked the sidelines in street clothes.

"Oh, we were tough, all right, and now and then I might break a tackle, but there were no miracles on that practice field. Sometimes, when we lined up against the first-team defense, my blockers looked like a flimsy fence in front of a bunch of wild boars being goaded by these nasty assistant coaches. When I hit the line, maybe twenty times a scrimmage, it sounded like mating season, but only one side was enjoying it. I actually heard guys yell junk like 'I got me something sweet that time.'"

Mr. F's eyes got lost in the TV. "The worst side of taking licks on the scout team was those hits set you apart from yourself and others. You didn't exactly strut down Dickson Street, saying, 'Look at me! I got whipped today.' When survival is your only goal, it drains your spirit. What Daddy said almost came true. We were cannon fodder with privileges: the school gave us great food, top medical treatment, and the chance to get an education, that is if you cared. But most scouts were in a fog.

"It made some guys get weird. They belched like machine guns or lit farts with matches. We had a guy called 'Cellblock' because of his black stubble and flat eyes. He stuffed his meals down his throat and then he mixed up people's leftovers and ate the mishmash. If you tried to leave the table with something on your plate, Cellblock's hand locked on you till you gave up the tray."

While we talked, the Falcons edged back into the game. A receiver caught a ball behind his back, and Mr. F and I shouted.

From the back of the house, Rae yelled, "One person here is trying to study!"

"We'll hold it down," Mr. F said to placate her, but he was excited. "By God, that catch reminds me of Purtman."

"Purtman?"

"Johnny, you never heard of him, but you could have. He was best pass receiver I ever saw. But he was a scout. Never played one down in a Razorback game. He could have been a star, but a coach started dogging him when he was a freshman because he supposedly wouldn't practice with a minor injury. This coach poisoned the other coaches' minds. He said, 'Purtman just can't strap it on.' That line followed Purtman around like a curse.

"You should have seen him before practice, catching balls one-handed and every which way. He made fools of first-teamers, but the scouts didn't pass much because most of our opponents had conservative offenses. Purtman had another problem, if you want to call it that: Girls went wild for those nimble hands of his. He missed curfew. Instead of giving Purtman a little slack or trying to help him or even just running him off, the coaches used him like tent-show preachers do a convenient sinner. 'Look at Purtman,' they told all of us. 'He just couldn't strap it on.' Boys got the message."

As I left the Futrelles that afternoon, dusk flared, stunning my eyes as if I'd just left a theater. For once, the connection between football and the game of life wasn't a coach's cliché. Throughout that fall, as he told me the rest of his story, I was more impressed by Mr. F's endurance than I would have been if he had spun a tale of glory.

Golden Gate

You're probably wondering, as I did at first, why Mr. F told his story to a high school boy he was only getting to know. One answer was obvious: Isolated by race and position, he had no one else to talk to in town except Rae, and, as I came to find out later, she wasn't interested. He couldn't have befriended an employee at the plant without creating envy. In Spinkville, there was no black man to go fishing with him. His wife, busy in Detroit, already knew his story.

Throughout that fall, hearing him talk, I realized he had always been a listener. Based on what he told me about growing up with hard-working parents in Drumlin, he had fallen into step, becoming an obedient boy who kept to himself. I'd guess that quiet people yearn to be heard, more and more, as time passes. The desire to open up had surely mounted in Mr. F. The past haunted him that fall perhaps because he was back in Arkansas, where football was inescapable and a giant of a bass had landed him someone with common interests who wanted to hear what he had to say.

I, too, had never been much of a talker, even though, young as I was, I wanted to honestly tell the truth of my experience to someone. That's what I'm trying to do now by talking to you. How would I have felt if I'd kept myself inside till I was middle-aged? Although Mr. F seemed almost ego-less to me—except for that money clip and his stylish clothes, which were like business cards—he must have seen the worth in his story. Most everybody wants to be known.

Early one Sunday morning, driving us to Lake Wedington, near Fayetteville, he said, "There was a time in my life when I never wanted to see these roads again, and here I am, Johnny."

We bought bait, lugged our tackle to a shady point, and fished, lines whizzing way out, catching and releasing baby bream and little catfish that looked almost cute. The fish were so small we had to ease the hook out of their mouths to keep from mutilating them. Otherwise, when we threw them back, they'd turn

Michael Gaspeny

belly-up.

"I feel sorry for the little ones," I said, and, for a change, I told Mr. F a story. "See that dock across the lake? When I was a kid, I was fishing there one morning. The only other fisherman was a stupid man who kept catching fish tiny as the ones we're throwing back. Little finger perch, hooked deep. When he reeled them in, he cussed, ripped the hook out, and tossed the fish in the trash barrel. You could see the little strands of bones dangling from their lips in that barrel along with the rotting bait and beer bottles. They looked like they were mumbling. It made me sad.

"The man noticed. He said, 'Son, those are trash-fish, and they are *my* fish. I caught 'em. They might as well have my name on 'em, and you might as well get used to it.' I felt like telling him, 'I hope a shark catches you one day,' but I just reeled in and left."

Mr. F said, "That's a sin twice over. He shouldn't have killed anything he wasn't going to eat or display, and if he'd thrown the little ones back, they could have fattened up for us to catch today."

Mr. F had a waste-not, want-not outlook. He wanted to be useful and he wanted to put the world to use. A big part of his story was how he got that way.

He said, "I've never been gut-hooked, but I have felt like

nothing. When I was on the scout team, I walked around in a daze at night, all over the place. I knew the bullfrogs out here by name. I talked to cows in the fields. By my junior year, I wasn't doing a thing but sleeping and walking, sometimes at the same time.

"I was failing an English course. The coaches assigned me a new tutor, when the old one complained about my motivation. The problem was I couldn't think of anything to write about. One day a plum-dark girl with a fast walk and a briefcase whipped into the lobby of the football dorm, and when guys gave her the eye, she glared like they were roaches. I met her in a study room. Her name was Tahirah Hayes. She looked at the topic for my next essay—*Something I Do in My Spare Time*—and gave me that glare.

'This isn't a joke, is it?' she asked.

'No,' I said.

'You should be writing about more important things,' she said. 'All right, what do you do away from the field?'

'Wander around.'

'OK. That's something—*The Wanderings of Charley Futrelle*. Be honest. Don't write what you think someone wants to hear. Put your heart into it.'"

Mr. F looked out at the lake as if Tahirah Hayes were

Michael Gaspeny

crossing the water. "You know, Johnny, when you like somebody, you remember everything about that person. While I wrote, she read *The Fire Next Time* by James Baldwin. I didn't know who he was. I wrote about how the tree frogs shrieked out here at Wedington and the time I tripped over a couple of lovers on the ground. I included how people passing in cars on the highway yelled at me. I mentioned the lost souls and sad sacks I met on the road.

"I gave her the paper. She read it twice, the second time jotting notes. Between readings, she sat up a little straighter.

"She wanted to know what people yelled.

'I don't want to offend you.'

'I asked you to tell me.'

'*Nigger* this and that. Black guys call me *Punk*. Some girls call me *Tramp* or *Bama*. Other girls say they're going to get me in the car and pass me around.'

'Write it,' she said. 'Tell how it makes you feel.'

"She went back to James Baldwin. When she read the second draft, her pen started scratching. Then she said, 'I want you to listen to yourself,' and I thought, 'Now you're going to get it.' She read something like this: 'The shouts jolt the back of my neck. My shoulders jump like a scared cat's. Then I feel empty because people made me do something I didn't want to do. They go on whooping down the road.'

'That's good,' she said. 'Time's up. I have to go. Revise it and add one more thing: Explain what your wanderings mean. See you at the same time tomorrow.'

"She left so fast I barely got the thank-you out of my mouth. And then, Johnny, remember that old trick where kids sneak up on your porch, ring the bell, and run away before you get to the door? What she asked me to explain pestered me like that bell. I went to the door, but all I saw were the bushes swaying in the breeze.

"Then, after practice, I walked into the shower, turned on the water, and the answer struck me in the face: 'What my wanderings mean is I'm always by myself.'

"Next day, she liked what I wrote, gave me a few pointers about grammar, and asked, 'What do you do on the scout team?'

'Run plays, take a beating.'

'Why?'

'Scholarship.'

'You get hit in exchange for an education?'

'For a walk, until recently.'

"She got up and said, 'I hope you can walk after you graduate.'

"She started to go. I felt desperate. I asked, 'Would you take a walk with me sometime?'

'It's against the rules. Besides, I'm occupied.'

"I asked a dumb question—'What keeps you so busy?'

'I try to make a difference,' she said. 'Here, walk with this,' and gave me *The Fire Next Time*.

"Oh, she was occupied, all right—head of Black Cultural Awareness, organizing events left and right. When I got a 'B+' on the essay, I went to the BCA office to thank her. The place was packed. She was rounding up volunteers to help with an NCAAP convention coming to town. I signed up.

"There were events and events to come. She was always out there fighting against something—the war in Vietnam, police brutality, apartheid, poverty. She led the drive for a Black Studies Program. I didn't have a thing to offer her but energy. I put up posters, circulated petitions, flipped pancakes in church kitchens, worked as a marshal during demonstrations. But what I mostly did was watch her from the end of a long line. Politicians, visiting professors, basketball players, preachers, Black Panthers—all tried to hit on her. But their moves were wasted because, except for business, she wouldn't give a man a glance.

"She didn't laugh, joke, tease, or flirt. Men, dope, alcohol, tobacco—all forbidden. She was in charge and always charging. Coffee was her only close friend. I kept a cup near her all the time, but I didn't try to distract her. She was made for forward motion—and you had best not get in the way. And she wouldn't eat! Even at banquets, she just nibbled like an insect on spinach leaves, a crouton here and there. Picnics, it was yellow celery with crusty pimento cheese, stale cookies. She started to get big-eyed and skinny.

"One day I was cooking at a breakfast fundraiser for BCA. I set a plate of scrambled eggs and country sausage next to her coffee.

'Breakfast smells nauseate me,' she said.

'How about a sandwich?' I asked.

'More coffee and plenty of space.'

'You can't save the world if you starve to death.'

'That's what they're doing in Ireland,' she said. 'I'm not hungry. Take that away.'

"Everyone called her 'T.' 'T,' I said, 'you're wasting away.' And here I made a near fatal mistake. I told her, 'It's like watching a work of art disappear.'

"She bolted up, planted her hands on her hips, and got up in my face like she was going to bite me, said, 'I don't tolerate talk

Michael Gaspeny

like that. Keep this up and you can go back to wandering.'

"Then in the middle of one May night, she called and asked if I had a driver's license. I did. Hers had been suspended for repeated speeding. No surprise there! She wanted a teeny favor—for me to drive her and two administrators from Prairie Grove College to an Anti-Poverty conference in San Francisco. Whoa! You know, I'd never been out of Arkansas, except once for a high school scrimmage in Louisiana. Johnny, I'm ashamed to say I never thought twice about my lack of travel.

"I took the wheel. I hope to never see the likes of Doctors Woller and Shipton again. They wore wigs—one satin black, the other maple—traveled in silk dresses and high heels. They addressed each other as 'Doctor,' even though they'd known each other since childhood. They pronounced every syllable of every word. Nothing suited them—not the climate inside or out, my driving, or T's taste for gospel music on the radio. They approved of classical music only. In their opinion, too many black folk had the gospel addiction, and the bass guitar was Satan's favorite instrument.

"The doctors refused to eat fast food. They insisted on going to Holiday Inns, which they pronounced 'Hullady Een,' like Scottish people on TV. At the restaurants, the waiters and waitresses couldn't move fast enough. The doctors blamed the slow service from whites on prejudice and from blacks on trifling.

"All they talked about was 'grahnts,' as in 'grants' from corporations or the government for their projects. Johnny, those doctors were getting to me like a smoking cigarette butt eating into a car seat.

"Quick into the trip, T. made the places we passed into a travelogue. Joplin, Missouri was Langston Hughes' birthplace. She said he rebelled against his father, who hated his own race. Once, when they were on a train passing cotton-pickers, the father called the field hands 'beasts.' Right then, Langston Hughes swore to love his people, no matter the cost.

"Outside Kansas City, which had been a great jazz town where Charlie 'Bird' Parker cut his teeth, she told a story about how he got his nickname. During the Depression, he and his band were driving across Kansas when he spotted a dead chicken in the road. He wanted to stop and see if the chicken was fresh enough to pluck and fry. So the guys started calling him 'Bird.'

"The doctors said Langston Hughes told a little too much about the secrets of the people he supposedly loved. They criticized Charlie Parker for dragging down his race by being a drug addict.

Michael Gaspeny

"As we crossed the Plains, T. talked about Crazy Horse riding himself into a trance before battles and the cavalry starving Indians by slaughtering buffalo. She loved knowledge. There was a hush in her voice that got the doctors off my mind for a little while.

"After one dinner out west, the doctors stiffed the waitress. When they went to the rest room, I put some money on the table. T. and I went outside and stood in the sun. I said, 'The light out west's different from Arkansas. It makes everyone look like a trophy.'

'No humidity,' T. said.

"Across the road, some cowboys in Stetson hats jumped out of a pick-up truck and strutted into a liquor store. The sun brushed their shoulders. 'Real cowboys!' I said. 'The only ones I've ever seen were on TV.'

'You could be one,' she said. 'Strong and steady.'

"I checked behind us before I said, 'I wouldn't mind saying *Adios* to those doctors. They're worse than bossy white women.'

'Where do you think they learned? They prove our old saying, "We have to be twice as good to get half as much,"' T. said.

"Her mind packed a wallop. She could have knocked me

down. When that happens, you know it's the truth. Just then, the doctors came out and looked askance at me. I noticed my shirt had puffed out of my pants.

"Later, right about dusk, I was driving, T. reading, the doctors jabbering. I spotted something that looked like a cane lying in the middle of the highway. It snapped under the wheel, a piece flying up behind the car. I saw an arm rise from the brush along the road.

'There's somebody back there!' I yelled, slowing down, pulling over, turning on the flashers.

"The doctors protested. I sprinted down the highway. Sure enough, a heavy white man with a bloody head moaned in the weeds. I lifted him, trying to run, but he weighed me down to a waddle. T. jumped out and opened the door to the back seat where the doctors grumbled.

'Get in front!' I told them. They didn't budge. 'All right then, I'll dump him in your laps and let him bleed all over your dresses.'

"That got them moving. I told T. to drive back to town, where I'd seen a sign for a hospital. I heaved the man in, propped him up, and T. took off. Blood coated his forehead and cheeks. I tore off my tee shirt and bound his head. The car flew. His pulse was lagging.

"Right then, I saw a serious problem: What kind of re-action awaited a shirt-less black guy hauling a bloody white man into an emergency room in the Land of Mormons who had more guns than they did kids? Suddenly, Johnny, it flashed in my head that the doctors could be an advantage to me.

"T. squealed up to the emergency room entrance. I said, 'All of you follow me in there. If not, we might never get to San Francisco.'

"I hoisted the man and staggered inside, shouted, 'We found this man beside the road!'

"A doctor and nurse came running as I eased the man onto a gurney. A fat guard sidled around the corner, with a pistol and a walkie-talkie on his belt. He sized me up.

"I said, 'You don't think I harmed this man with these three ladies watching, do you?'

"One look at the women told him the truth. I said, 'I don't know who he is or where he came from. I wish him the best, but I hope to never see him again!'

"I hurried the women out of there and put on a fresh shirt while the wigs returned to the judge's chambers in the back seat. I got behind the wheel, wanting to floor the car, but I crept out of that town. All I heard was breathing for a while, and then T. slid a tape into the deck.

'What's that?' I asked.

'John Coltrane, *Giant Steps.* '

"She looked over, caught the corner of my eye, said, 'By the way, Charley, I know he wasn't heavy, because he was your brother!'

"She laughed for the first time since I'd met her and turned up the music. That made me feel pretty good.

"When we reached the hotel in San Francisco, I felt like I'd been released from jail. I got restless in my room and hit the streets, no idea where I was going. The Golden Gate Bridge rose over the city like a stage. It drew me through the Marina District and all those sailboats and yachts, then to Fort Point. I felt excited. I climbed the hill above the fort, taking a path through the trees. The bridge was almost in my face. I walked up a ramp. I couldn't believe the Golden Gate Bridge was so open. I had only seen it on TV, and it seemed as far away from Drumlin, Arkansas as the moon.

"Then I was on the bridge, looking back at Alcatraz, 'The Rock' they called it in the movies. I ran to the other side of the bridge, nearly got hit by a cab. I grabbed a cable and looked out at the Pacific. I'd never seen an ocean. Deep down inside, I had just accepted that this bridge and every ocean belonged to other people, all white except for black celebrities, approved by whites. But I was there now, and it was mine, too, and everybody's. All you needed was a little luck and the will to get there. So all those hits on the practice field, all my so-called wanderings led me to T. and the bridge. She had a camera, and I wanted to come back in the daytime and have her take a picture that I could send home to Daddy.

"I walked all over the waterfront straight into the sun. When I got back to the hotel, T. was fuming in the lobby. She got up in my face and said, 'So when you hit the bright lights, you just start running the streets?'

"That stung me. I said, 'I was sight-seeing, not running the streets. What business is it of yours?'

'After your history of night walks?'

"I told her, 'I haven't done that kind of walking since I met you. But, no matter what I was doing, everybody's got to get out sometime. Including you.'

'I won't argue in the lobby,' she said. 'It's trashy.'

"We went outside and entered the first place that seemed private, a restaurant on Pier 38. Off the balcony, sea lions rolled and slid on rafts hitched to the docks.

"The waiter came, and I ordered two black coffees and two glasses of red wine. T. looked at me like I was crazy. I told her, 'If you don't want your wine, I'll drink 'em both. If you don't watch out, you're going to end up like the doctors.'

"She fetched the longest sigh I ever heard. 'I am already getting like the doctors,' she said. 'Slavery and Jim Crow won't leave me alone. White people say, "It's all even now because we have given you rights, affirmative action, and welfare." How could it ever be even? Those so-called gifts can't split open the earth and bring our people back to life. Charley, it's on me night and day.'

"I listened closely, but I was also watching the sun glow on the sea lions as they snouted one another off the rafts. The wine and coffee came. She sipped the coffee and tasted the wine.

'Here's how severe my case is,' she said. 'Instead of listening to the sea lions barking and the cable cars clanging, I'm down home hearing these white men snicker and say, "If you've ever been a nigger on Saturday night, you'll never want to be white again." But, Charley, where is the fun? How'd you like to spend Saturday nights like the doctors? Are you having fun on the scout team? Do you think the people sleeping in the alleys around

Michael Gaspeny

here are enjoying their accommodations? If you ask me, white people are having almost all the fun. And it doesn't do me any good when you disappear, because I have grown to like knowing where you are.'

"I wanted to cheer, but I just said, 'We need something to eat.'"

Mr. F stood and packed up his tackle box. I was a little slow to move. I felt like I was shaking myself awake. A strange thing had happened in my mind: Rae and I replaced Tahirah Hayes and Charley Futrelle at the table above the sea lions. She was saying nice things to me. I called the waiter.

Lee's Lounge

Three days after that fantasy, the news struck me like a helmet in the gut. The blow came on a Wednesday, "Woden's Day," named for the Nordic god of the gallows, according to Ms. Colwin. In World Lit, she announced: "For the first time ever, Spinkville High is sending a student to an Ivy League school. Rae Futrelle has been accepted at Princeton University. For the earphone-heads among you, Princeton is located in New Jersey. It's where Albert Einstein taught. Although Rae has been with us for only a brief time and we cannot share the credit for this achievement, we can bask in her reflected glory."

As the class applauded, I wanted to shout, "I want to bask in her arms!" The students' response was touching. No one had befriended her, nor had she condescended to make a friend, but the good-natured class recognized accomplishment by anyone among our number. Rae's brilliance could not be denied. Her title of "Know-It-All" had lost its bite and come true. She seemed surprised, even slightly pleased by the clapping. Her face warmed toward a smile, the good will in the room challenging her bias against a hick town. I felt sour. My relationship with Rae would end before it ever began. In less than a year she would study under a bust of Einstein, and I would be even farther from her consideration.

Who do you love? I heard the Bo Diddley song all day in my head. After school, I ducked Missy and followed Rae out the door. I wanted to say something, anything that might get her attention. But middle-school kids blocked me from Rae, all sporting "Grab a Grand" badges, wanting my signature below their names. Rae disappeared among the school buses. It was as if she had swept into the future, while I was stuck in the past. I signed the badges as neatly as I could.

Everything seemed wrong. There was one me giving out his autograph, sticking with Missy, and obeying Coach Chuck Hurd, and there was another wanting to take a hand-off, run clear out of the stadium, and throw himself at Rae's feet. It was high time to return to Lee's Golden Lounge, no matter how abusive the proprietor became. Lee's was the only place I could experiment with my second self.

When I arrived, he was doing one-hand push-ups while Jim Morrison sang "Backdoor Man." It seemed strange to me that Willie Dixon had written this song that became a classic tune for Howlin' Wolf and was covered by The Doors so that a quarter of a century later, a body-building goat-boy who hated the past could pump through workouts. If America was a melting pot, it was also a melted clock, and, from what I knew of our nation's sins, that dead clock was a curse.

I said, "You ought to rename this place 'Lee's Blue Lounge.'"

"What blues? Your brains are as blue as your balls," Lee said, uncapping forties for us.

I told him more than enough about Chester Arthur Burnett, a.k.a. Howlin' Wolf, who plowed fields in West Memphis, Arkansas until he was almost forty. Then he cut some songs at Sam Phillips' Memphis Recording Service, and headed north. I included how the gigantic Wolf, who weighed three hundred pounds, threw himself to the floor in West Side Chicago clubs, growling and moaning. I asked Lee who was more of a man, Chester Burnett or Jim Morrison, suburbanite son of a naval commander.

"It's not an either/or situation," Lee said. "You're starting to rave and you just got here."

I glugged from that forty. "I'm raving at me, too. What right do I have to the blues? Here I am a Caucasian member of the first family of Spinkville singing along with Son House on 'Death Letter.' What do I know about being up against the wall? The only thing haunting me is a bad crush. If I don't live the life, what right do I have to the music? Is it just a cheap way to pick up some color?"

"Why are you so hung up on purity? You can't be somebody else."

"That's not what you said the last time I was here. The senseis always say, 'Get yourself out,' remember?"

"Don't take it personally."

"How else am I supposed to take it?"

Sick of his double-talk, I was sicker of myself. My moodswings had become as sudden as his. In fact, I was pissed with everything. Lee started pumping iron, while I tried to settle down. I hung around for a while, feeling twisted, trying not to like The Doors and thumbing through his *Kama Sutra* until I finished my forty and took off.

On the way home, I hated myself. I had an all-consuming craving to leave Spinkville until I got myself right. My flesh was stinking hot; I reeked like lighter fluid as I undressed for bed. Where would I go? New Orleans was too far away. I had read that Beale Street in Memphis had become a tourist trap. The Windy City and the Mississippi Delta were meccas for blues pilgrims. I often fantasized about shouting in a South Side Chicago lounge while Muddy Waters bellowed "Long Distance Call" and squeezed those piercing notes out of his slide guitar. But he died in 1983, and I didn't have the street-sense to navigate the South Side, and, besides, Chicago was too far away. The Delta was another matter: though it lay all the way across the state, I could drive there, have a blinding night, and get back in twenty-four hours. I fell asleep, seeing myself on the banks of the Mississippi.

Having an escape lifted my spirits. I didn't feel happy or optimistic, but my skin stopped sickening me. I wanted to live honestly, square with myself, and to act out of my true feelings instead of pleasing others. That fall I had learned I did not want to spend the rest of my days in Spinkville or marry Missy, no matter how highly I regarded her. I was football king, she Homecoming queen. We had ridden a float through town since kindergarten, guided by the remote control of social class. Until Rae came to

Spinkville, I was a happy sleepwalker; now I had run smack into the wall. I wanted to break up with Missy, and yet I had to do it right. Out of respect for her goodness and our long, happy comfort, I had to let her down easy, even though I knew that wasn't possible. My calculation seems cynical now, but how else do you end a marriage from the cradle?

In the morning, I fetched *The Mountain Eagle*, flipped to the sports page, and under the headline "It All Starts With a Thousand," this was the opening of Tate Donner's column: "The word 'thousand' has a windy sound as it leaves the tongue. If you don't believe me, say it to yourself right now: 'Thou-sand.' It's the haunting sound of opportunity. Johnny Spink has heard that wind all season long. Soon he can make the word his own."

I read no further. Dad brought plates of scrambled eggs, bacon, and toast to the table and took in the column with a glance. He could read a hundred pages an hour with ninety-five percent comprehension. He said, "Tate's sure blowing the bugle this morning."

"I hate it," I answered. "It would be bad enough if the record meant something, but this whole business is phony."

"Uneasy rests the crown on the king's head."

It was the wrong thing to say to me that day. I snapped,

"I'm not a king, Dad. You're doing what Tate did."

"Just a figure of speech."

I looked away and made a face.

"Anyway, it will soon be over," Dad said.

I wanted to yell, "And then what?"

I knew what he expected me to do. I also knew the Esmeraldo game might never be over for me. It would bleed into the rest of my life.

Missy's Taurus appeared in the driveway. It was our day to ride to school together. Getting into the car, fuming over Dad's remarks, I didn't want to kiss her, but I did.

"How did you feel about Tate's column?" she asked.

"It made me so ill I couldn't get past the first paragraph," I said. "It's an epidemic."

"Let's skip school today," she said.

"What!" I exclaimed. I had never known her to break a rule except for one time. It left her guilty, and from then on, we always pulled back.

"Let's go to Tulsa to the zoo. What can they do to us?"

"Nothing," I replied. That was the truth. "Until I suit up for the Esmeraldo game, I can do whatever I want. You can always do what you want."

Michael Gaspeny

What a hypocrite I was! I had gone to bed wanting to break up with Missy, and now we were ditching school and heading west to Tulsa. I tried to ease my conscience by claiming I needed to escape the elevens leaping on those "Grab a Grand" badges and the echoes of Tate's column. But that was an evasion. I was too weak to be honest, although I have to admit that Missy's sudden rebelliousness interested me.

The day was another golden gift from an Indian Summer more stunning than any I could remember. In the dry, bright weather, leaves kept to the trees, curling in apricot and apple colors. Missy asked me to drive. She found a classic rock station on the radio—compromise music. We were off by ourselves on back roads flashing down the twisting flume of hills on the hundred mile ride to Tulsa. When Cream's version of "Crossroads" came on, I resisted lecturing about Robert Johnson. Missy drew up close to me. One thing led to another, as almost never happened with us. The shiny road and glowing foliage jumped in my eyes. I stopped thinking.

Way back in the hills, near the Oklahoma border, Missy told me to pull over. She grabbed a blanket, and we walked over a rise, down into a forest that rushed in reddish-gold waves from one hill to another as far as you could see. The fragrance from the hot leaves under our feet became incense tasting like black soil. Missy went ahead of me into the gushing light. It looked, I swear, like the breath of the earth. Suddenly she took off her top and draped it over a branch, and then, farther into the woods, she hung something on a twig, and something else until she had made a trail of her clothes. I could barely breathe. I collected the gifts she left along the way.

I understand now there was calculation in what she did, but what courage it took for her to leap so far from her nature. As I held her, she said, "We don't have to be what our parents and the town want. We don't have to be bored, Johnny. I want you to be who you really are with me. Don't be afraid."

Yes, we finally got to the zoo. The lions, grizzlies, and polar bears were the drabbest part of the day. On the way home, we returned to the woods and crushed each other again. It seemed like we could have gone on and on like that. About the time we hit Spinkville, a song we both liked played on the radio, Eric Clapton's version of "Tulsa Time," and we shouted along. When we reached my driveway, I had to pull myself from her. I had started the day not loving Missy, and now, whether I loved her or not, I was stunned by her. Maybe all along I had been the somnambulist (one of Ms. Colwin's ten-dollar words) in the relationship, and

Michael Gaspeny

Missy was wide awake.

Dad had left a note saying he'd flown to Memphis on business. The phone rang. Coach Chuck Hurd harangued me about being AWOL from practice.

"I needed a personal day, Coach, to commune with nature."

There was nothing he could do to me, except utter a few impotent warnings. I said good night.

Now that Missy and I were back in Spinkville, the magic faded. We put on our old roles. I could have tried to rekindle the flame. I could have been who I wanted to be with her, but I had identity problems. With my celebrity and her projects, we were as tense in town as we had been free in the woods.

That Friday night, I felt heavy and listless before the Chinquapin game. Then, during the first quarter, a kid put a hit on me that caused my lights to flicker like power during a thunderstorm. The jolt made me weak-kneed for a flash, but it woke me up, too. This might sound deranged, but sometimes a good, hard lick released me from my mind and into the sensations of the game—in this case, a back-and-forth clash with both teams piling up touchdowns. By the last minute, even though I had scored four times and Lee twice, we were down by a point. Our undefeated season—the first in Spinkville history—was about to die.

We had the ball on our own 30. During our last time-out, I went wild raving about how we hadn't come this far to lose out on our dream, how it was gut-check time and we were going to leave it all on the field. You name the cliché; I shouted it. Coach Chuck gave us instructions and shoved me toward the line of scrimmage. The play he called was a pitch to the right with me trying to burst around end. Now Robert Joyner, our tight end, had ADD, and sometimes he wandered offside before the snap. He was a fierce blocker, but when he lost focus, you might find him anywhere on the field. So I swung right, taking the pitch, and dodged one tackler in the flat. Five or six tacklers veered in my direction when something caught my eye downfield, Robert Joyner, trotting, looking lost in all that space. He hadn't caught a pass all year. In fact, the tight end never figured into our feeble passing schemes, and neither did I. Also, Robert had the thickest, deadest hands on the team, as our coach loved to point out. But when I spotted Robert's lazy lope, it was like I was playing backyard football. I instinctively slung the ball downfield.

It landed on Robert's navel at about the Chinquapin 30,

Michael Gaspeny

and then the ball tried to slither away, down his wrists and over his palms and nearly off his fingertips and then back to his belly and out again, and he juggled it into the end zone where he finally hugged the ball. I looked for flags because often when you pass from a running play, there's danger of an ineligible receiver downfield, but nobody except Robert had trespassed beyond the line of scrimmage, and he was a legitimate receiver. So we won on a sandlot play.

As a kid, now and then I was seized by high spirits for no reason at all, and I skipped across a schoolyard or down a sidewalk, heedless of social opinion. The touchdown pass to Robert Joyner revived that old feeling. I felt free as a black Labrador soaring to snag a spinning Frisbee. It's hard to skip in cleats, but I leaped and floated.

My elation didn't last much longer than my post-game shower. As Missy and I drove through town and parked on a country road, the glow of the game faded as she complained about rivalries among the cheerleaders and the frustrations of raising money for the senior trip, et cetera. She was just getting tuned up. At one time, I would have drifted beyond her chatter, but the open spaces in my mind had closed. I tried to distract her with a kiss, but she pulled away.

"I want you to listen to me," she said.

"Sorry. I am listening. But I've heard all this before."

"All right then, you talk."

"I don't have anything to say."

"That always means you're afraid to say what's really on your mind."

She was right. At least I could mention one of my problems. "I can't get away from this business about the record. I'll feel better after the Esmeraldo game."

"What are you going to do?"

"Maybe shoot off my little toe."

"That's not funny. This is a serious situation. People love you here. You have responsibilities."

"So you're telling me what to do? Join the crowd, Missy. Dad, Ms. Colwin, even Mr. Futrelle is leaning that way."

"Really? I thought he'd tell you to go fishing during the Esmeraldo game."

"What? Mr. Futrelle's the most responsible man in Spinkville. You don't like him, do you?"

"He seems nice enough, I don't really know him, and you won't share him."

"People need their private side."

Michael Gaspeny

"Is that where you keep Rae? I see the way you look at her."

So that was what all her blather about cheerleaders had been hiding.

"I need some privacy." I declared, starting the car. "I'm taking you home now."

"Oh, then, you won't talk about it?"

"I'm finishing sharing for tonight."

"Well, I'm not," Missy said and whacked me against the temple. It was an open-handed blow, but it packed a pent-up fury and came without a warning. My head hummed.

"Now you can take me home," she said. "You better come to your senses, boy!"

The Kiss

I took my slapped face home, logged onto the Internet, and typed "blues." I needed to get away for awhile—even if it was just in my imagination. Before long, I was in the Delta, taking a blues tour of Clarksdale, Mississippi, the streets mapped out, the juke joints designated by stars. Six or seven clubs appeared with names like Margaret's Blue Diamond Lounge and the King Snake, all looking so close together that you could walk from one to another. And I saw the holy ground of Stovall Plantation where Muddy Waters had worked the fields and developed his sound. Nearby in Helena, Arkansas, the Delta Blues Museum had the fabled sign from the juke joint where Robert Johnson died of pneumonia after being poisoned by a man he cuckolded.

Michael Gaspeny

Disappearing into the map, I imagined the clubs as a blues history, leading from the Delta acoustic masters to pounding Southside Chicago blues to the jazz-like artistry of T-Bone Walker and B.B. King to a far-out Jimi Hendrix disciple playing slide guitar from Venus. I printed the maps and secured them in the back of my World Lit notebook. When I got frustrated, I mused over Clarksdale. The names of the streets and clubs shone like images in a prized poem. I saw new possibilities with every reading.

On Sunday, while Mr. F and I fished at Lake Wedington, the sky darkened, wind thrashed the trees, and he yelled, "It looks like what happened after they crucified Jesus!" I rushed the tackle boxes to the car, and Mr. F. limped after me with the rods. The storm struck, but we caught only the edge, and we left the thunderclaps behind us. Riding through Fayetteville, Mr. F. spotted Roger's Recreation Hall and said, "I always wanted to go in there when I was a scout, but it was off-limits. Let's shoot a game of pool."

For the first time, I had been somewhere he hadn't because Lee Branch had introduced me to Roger's last summer. But I didn't say so. We parked on Dickson Street and headed inside the old school pool room—a cave with yellow tile walls, concrete floor, bar in front, topped with jars of hot sausages and pickled pig's feet. The dim realm contained a hodge-podge of beer banners, Razorback memorabilia, caricatures of customers, and photos of high times. But no jukebox. Music was banned. You were supposed to talk to people, trade wisecracks, and swap stories. Stepping into Roger's, you left the year behind and entered a shrine from the Depression. I could feel ghosts nursing beers and finding a laugh during hard times.

The bartender called "Coach" had a bristling handlebar moustache and a robust welcome. We got a tray of pool balls, bought soft drinks and snacks. Mr. F didn't touch alcohol. Once he told me, "Fifty percent of most folks' problems come right out of the bottle." The percentage rose to ninety percent when my father and mother had been together. Mr. F paid from his money clip, but it didn't catch Coach's eye. At Roger's, nothing counted but good will. We took a table and tested the cues until we found ones to our liking. We sipped Dr. Peppers and crunched pork-rinds.

I racked the balls, Mr. F broke, and balls started falling. No matter the game—eight ball, nine ball, straight pool—he whipped me dizzy, never letting up—no flubbing shots or making encouraging remarks to give me hope. He wasn't showy; he didn't talk trash; he thought two or three shots ahead and wiped the floor with me. The man loved winning, maybe because he never had a chance to do so when he was a scout. I remembered the trophy bass on his office wall.

"You're a wizard," I said. "Where did you learn to play?"

"In scout days, when bad weather kept me from wandering, there was nothing to do at the football dorm except shoot pool or study. And you know what I did."

Then something struck me. I asked, "Mr. F, how did you get from there to here?"

He shook his head, saying, "That's a question I ask myself all the time. For one thing, I knew a lot about work. My father was always sticking a rake or axe in my hands, and my mother kept me busy with mops and brooms. Later, working at football was my ticket to college and T. I learned that the best thing a man can be is useful. But the answer to your question began one morning after football season my senior year. An assistant coach poked his head into my room and said, 'Charley, Coach Carson wants to see you.'

'Me?'

'You, son.'

"Coach hadn't spoken to me since the day I signed my scholarship papers. Oh, but I'd seen him for four years on his tower above the practice field—God with a megaphone. When I started with the scouts, I hoped to make a great run and have him come down from on high and glorify me, but I got that foolishness knocked out of me fast.

"On the way to see him, I had the jitters. I wondered if my link with T and politics had caused trouble. The BCA demonstrations got media attention. Sometimes there was a scrape. The cameras caught me once or twice. You know how backward this state can be. The Razorbacks were turning darker and darker. Some of the boosters still didn't like it and called the team 'The Razorblacks.' Bigots like them love for a black man to get into trouble. I wondered if I had embarrassed the program. Image was everything at Arkansas. Coach Carson's operation was scandal-free, squeaky-clean. I thought he might send me packing. I saw my suitcase on the curb outside the football dorm.

"In his office, Coach led me to the window over the practice field. He said, 'I want you to know how much we appreciate your effort down there. I know it's been a lot of sweat and pain, but you have made yourself a member of the Razorback family, and, Charley, at Arkansas, we don't forget family.'

"I was confused. He seemed sincere, but he was also buttering my toast. 'By the way,' he said, 'there's a gentleman who wants to meet you.'

"I wondered if this was a set-up. The door of an inner of-

Michael Gaspeny

fice opened, filled by a man big as a bronze elephant. You should have seen his clothes—soft-gold suit, aquamarine shirt, pearl-colored tie. Johnny, I was gob-smacked. When he said, 'We've been looking for you,' I thought he was an F.B.I. agent aiming to use me to get at T.

"He shook my hand and about broke my fingers even though I had a strong grip. He said, 'Call me Columbus. I represent Mr. Samuel Pitler. We're taking you to lunch today.'

"Sometimes, Johnny, you know things are out of your hands, and you just have to go along. On the elevator, I tried to keep my head. When we left the dorm, I saw a silver Rolls parked in the bowl below the stadium, all by itself. Columbus said, 'I hope you respect opportunity,' and opened the back door of the car.

"Shazam! There was the man I found along the road out west last summer—in the pink now, dressed in a pin-striped suit. He had a fleshy face, wavy silver hair, shrewd eyes. He said, 'At last I shake hands with my only outstanding debt. You saved my life. It's a wonder a load like me didn't break your back.'

"Columbus drove us downtown to the city club. When we walked in, people moved like pistons in a purring engine. The three of us sat down at a table with a reserved sign. Mr. Pitler said,

'Charley, you can give a man a fish or teach him how to fish.'

"That expression was new to me then. A waiter whispered something to Columbus. He left the table and came back with T in a shiny green dress. Oh, could she glorify green! Mr. Pitler and I stood as Columbus pulled out a chair for her.

"Mr. Pitler said, 'Here's the woman who brought us together.'

"As it happened, that guard at the hospital in Utah wrote down T's license plate number, and it had been typed on the admittance form.

"It turned out Mr. Pitler specialized in buying and reviving failing businesses. After we ate, he said, 'You know Columbus could use a protégé.' I didn't know what that word meant, but I didn't let on. Later, when T. and I were alone, she explained. 'A protégé is someone who receives guidance. Someone who gets taken under a beneficial wing.'

'I don't want to be anybody's bird,' I said, sounding like my father the night Jack DeRoza came to recruit me.

"She said, 'Everybody's somebody's bird until the bird takes off on its own. It means he's going to offer you a job after graduation. Listen to me: You saw him; you saved him; you deserve it! Do you think I and the doctors would have stopped?

We wouldn't have even seen him. I feel good about this. He's got presence you can't fake. He knows what's what. This is one white man worth learning from.' She squeezed my arm hard. Whatever made her happy was bound to please me.

"I asked, 'But how did a man like him get out there, pitched in the weeds?'

"T. said, 'That's a question you should never ask.' I didn't, and he never told me."

The Budweiser clock in Roger's read four. I broke a rack, scratched, and we quit shooting pool. I asked, "What do you think would have happened if you'd never met your wife and Mr. Pitler?"

Returning his cue to the stand, he said, "I would have become a Dickson dog or gone home to the lumber yard or straight into trouble. When you're wired to hit and get hit, it's hard to stop. Lord knows why, but the sun shined my shoes that day. I'll never forget when Columbus said: 'I hope you recognize opportunity.'"

Mr. F fiddled with his glasses, which had tortoise shell frames and looked special, like everything else about him. His every last detail reflected self-worth. Rae combined his pride and her mother's fire. He said, "Now you've got an opportunity, a big one."

It took me by surprise. I wanted to think about him, not me. Mr. F's stories gave me an escape, but this topic closed the theater.

"Setting the record's not like what you went through," I said.

"Right, but one thing Mr. Pitler taught me is when you walk down the street, you could become anyone you see. Life can make a beggar out of anybody. If you gain a thousand yards, that's like bonds in a safe deposit box. You'll always have that to fall back on."

For the first time in his company, there was an edge in my voice when I said, "I want to make my own investments."

"OK, I'm done preaching," he said. "Time to go home and get ready for Monday."

That week, Missy was absent from school for two days. Without her, I lined up for the bus taking the senior class on its annual trip to see a play at the university. Seniors from the hill towns all around converged on Fayetteville for the performance. As I boarded, a chant rose—"John-*ny*, John-*ny*!" My classmates stamped their feet and rocked the bus. The only empty seat was next to Rae, occupied by her purse and briefcase. Kids, intimidated by her, always gave Rae space. She reluctantly put her purse under her seat and the briefcase in her lap.

As I sat down, the bus took off. Rae sprang the lock on the briefcase, removed Toni Morrison's *Beloved*, and set the briefcase next to her right leg in between us. I envied the briefcase. She grew quickly absorbed in the novel, which we were studying in World Lit. I had what Ms. Colwin called "a linear mind," so the plot's fractured time sequence confused me. This must have been Rae's third time through the book, because there were already notes in different colored inks, and now she added a third.

At one time, my father hoped that I might become a scholar like he was. He could understand anything—from the law to chicken-processing to a Faulkner novel. The "A's" I made deceived him. I was a good student with a magnet-like memory, but I didn't have his mind. Teachers often gave me a few extra points for my family name, respectful manners, or athletic ability. Sitting next to Rae, with red leaves sailing by the bus and green ink gathering on her pages, I recalled a talk my father had once given me.

It came on one of our football weekends in Fayetteville. He spoke of the life of the mind and the privileges it could bring. As soon as I heard his measured tones, I tuned him out, but the message must have stuck. He said America always had a place for a smart achiever and such a person could live at a level of security above the scrambling lives so many people led. For a brief time in his fantasies, I resembled him. I racked up degrees, fellowships, and grants, made warm, beneficial associations, and had access to the ears of influential people. But as years passed and my touchdowns multiplied, those visions yielded to dreams of football glory.

I lacked the brain and will to become a professional scholar, but Rae was headed there. Her body rode a bus in a hick state bound for a play that wouldn't meet her standards, but her mind had already entered Princeton. She was ticketed for the good life my father had once envisioned for me. Knowing my time with her was running out, I felt a little bold.

"What's it like to be so smart?" I asked.

The intrusion irked her. "It's not hard to be smart in Spinkville," she said.

"You don't have to be from New York or Paris to be smart," I replied. "Or even Detroit. Didn't I notice that Toni Morrison's from Lorain, Ohio?"

"Yes."

"Not exactly a cultural mecca, I'd guess. You haven't answered my question."

She sighed dramatically. "Being smart is probably like having the skill to score touchdowns," she said. "But people don't rock the walls of the library when I check out a book."

I had never been close to Rae this long, except for the dinner at the Futrelles. It made me reckless. There were fifty other kids on the bus, but under the tent of their noise, it felt like we were alone.

I said, "You have a nice voice. I like the way you say things."

She laughed in surprise. "Save it for your better half."

"What I like is you don't just talk for the sake of talking. I can hear you thinking in the spaces between the words. But it's not the grinding way you hear teachers or parents thinking while they talk. You play inside your words. It's entertaining."

"Do you think it could possibly be offensive for a black woman to be told her talk is entertainment? I guess it's musical, too."

"It is musical."

"I need to read," she said.

In Fayetteville, a Homecoming festival had seized Dickson Street. Even at ten on a weekday morning, students crowded the pavement and cruised in horn-blasting cars. The high school buses were marooned in traffic. Kids opened the windows and called the Hogs—"Ooo, Pig, Sooie!" Homecoming was my father's favorite time of the year, superior to any holiday; he returned to his alma mater to hobnob with friends and bathe in nostalgia. The Razorbacks were our birthright, and Fayetteville our holy city. I felt like shouting along with my schoolmates.

"All this over a football game?" Rae said.

"That's only part of it. It's an excuse to party, like a little Mardi Gras."

"Pardon me, but it looks like a redneck round-up."

"Hey, I'm not a redneck. The people up here aren't, either. I took a blues-and-race course at the university. If I'm not mistaken, the black people out there look like they're having fun. Your dad and I were here last Sunday. He clobbered me at pool. Haven't you ever been to Fayetteville?"

"Why would I want to?"

I was shocked. "This is where your parents met. They used to walk these streets. Your dad got a degree by taking hits on the practice field. Your mom was an activist. No Fayetteville, no Rae."

I actually shut her up.

We finally reached the theater, a brand-new, multi-million dollar structure down the hill from the university. It was right in the middle of the festival. Mimes did routines; clowns roasted meat; artists drew caricatures. Our bus crawled into the parking lot, where kids zoomed from buses—beyond the control of teachers.

As Rae and I got off, I caught the spirit. "Let's skip the play," I yelled. I actually touched her back. "I'll show you around. Fayetteville has great bookstores. You ought to have at least one pleasant experience while you're in our state. They won't miss us."

"Ms. Colwin will see I'm gone."

"It doesn't matter. She thinks you raise the moon. You're going to Princeton. Let's go."

She had run out of "No's."

I took her to Rock Bottom Books where she found two Toni Morrison novels she wanted and I bought a new biography of Muddy Waters. We went to a sidewalk café for coffee and croissants and lounged in the sun, thumbing through our books.

Rae asked, "What's so great about Muddy Waters?"

I expounded. "He had it all. He was a brilliant country blues musician who learned from Delta masters like Son House.

He played a wicked slide guitar and had a huge voice. He went to Chicago and started playing electric guitar so he could be heard in noisy clubs."

"Did he rest on the seventh day?"

"No, he created the seven-man band, with drums, bass, piano, harmonica, first and second guitars, and vocalist. Call it a big rock band before rock ever existed. His groups had discipline and feeling. The members were so successful that they left Muddy to front their own bands. See, he was a genius at cultivating talent. Every ambitious bluesman wanted to play with him, from B.B. King to Eric Clapton."

My knowledge impressed her, even if it pertained to an inferior subject. "What makes a white boy in Spinkville love the blues so much?" she asked.

"The blues are deeper than other music."

She looked like an angler who had just gotten a strike. "So does that mean that black people lead deeper lives than whites?"

"Based on what I've read, I think most black people have been forced to look closer at the extremes of reality than the whites I know."

"And would that be true of me?"

"I don't really know you."

"Make me up. Guess who I am."

"You're proud, attractive, smart, ambitious. Maybe something like your mother."

"I'm not anything like my mother," she snapped.

"Sorry," I said, wondering if they were too much alike.

"Continue with my portrait."

I knew this was headed in a bad direction, but still I said, "In Detroit, you must have your choice of boyfriends."

"In Detroit, I don't have *any* boyfriends. A lot of men try to hit on me, but they're not looking for a smart girlfriend. And my mother disapproves of the boys who do come to the house. So I'm not exactly living on the edge, am I?"

"I guess not."

"By the way, how do *you* define reality? Isn't that *your* code word for primitivism and sexual gratification?"

I would not back down nor would I apologize for the music. "No, to me, reality means emergencies. White people like me have cushions against trouble. Look at the wealth gap. Look at all the gaps. And, yes, sex is the subject of lots of blues songs. Why wouldn't it be? During slavery, whites kept books out of black hands and worked their so-called property from dawn to sundown. What do you suppose slaves in the fields thought about while they were sowing and harvesting? Every form of freedom. I know where my mind goes when I feel confined."

I had read somewhere that girls thought about sex twice as often as boys did. I felt like asking what she thought about when *ennui* (another Colwin word) seized her, but Rae was probably eternally absorbed.

On this trip, with this opportunity, I would not hold back. "When I hear Robert Nighthawk play slide guitar, the notes sound like women's hips squiggling from the guitar. But blues are about so many other things, too. Like being hounded or trapped and surviving. They're about being proud and proving you're better than your circumstances. Some songs are mournful and ghostly, and others are hilarious."

"But I still don't understand why a rich white boy would be drawn to that music."

I hated to be called "rich." The truth hurts, but I swallowed my resentment. "Because the music moves me. I feel it. Maybe it reveals what's deep inside me—for better and worse. Maybe I'm trying to compensate for injustice. Whatever. What Muddy Waters calls 'deep blues' tell the truth about life. They hit me in the heart or the crotch or right between the eyes. I read books, I go to church, I try to crush people on the football field, but the blues are the truest thing I know."

I felt a little crazy. I seemed to be defending my existence. I tried to come back to sunny Dickson Street. "We've still got an hour and half. What else would you like to do?"

She felt the sun, too. "Let's go for a walk. I don't feel conspicuous here like I do in Spinkville. I love to walk."

I wanted to ask, "Where do you walk in Detroit?" There were so many questions I wanted to ask her.

When we joined the crowd on the sidewalk, I recognized three Esmeraldo football players hiding their incompetence inside Dallas Cowboy jerseys. They brushed past me, hissed a few taunts, and hurried off.

"What did those guys say?" Rae asked.

"Just the usual trash talk. They play for Esmeraldo. Our last game of the season's against them."

They represented the worst of the South and the last thing I wanted Rae to encounter in Fayetteville.

"They were making cracks about me, weren't they?"

I told her half of it. "No, they were threatening me. They're afraid I'm going to set a record against them."

"I heard something about burning. What did that mean?"

"They said they were going 'to burn me a new one.' That's

an idiotic figure of speech for the sexual torture of another male."

Rae fetched a heavy sigh. "We should have gone to the play," she said. "I knew something like this would happen."

"I'm sorry it happened, but let's have a good walk. This is a pretty town."

We strolled up the long, steep hill past the great oaks on the grounds of towering Old Main. I gave her a campus tour, pointing out the practice field where her father had made his sacrifices and the law school where my dad had studied. At Arkansas, it's custom to engrave each graduate's name in the sidewalk, and we found her parents' names near the library.

"The name project is always about three years behind, so I'll bet your parents have never seen their names here."

"I wish I had a camera," Rae said, for the first time approving of something about Arkansas other than Ms. Colwin.

It was hot and dry, with leaf-dust floating through the slashes of sun between the trees. We sat in the deserted amphitheater striped by shadows from the pines on the rise behind us. Rae turned her back to me.

"I'm sorry those guys threatened you," she said.

"It's nothing. But thanks."

The amphitheater encouraged contemplation. We were silent for awhile, but it wasn't uncomfortable. It was something we were sharing.

The day was so bright that the columns on stage seemed to pulsate. You could smell the resin in the pines. Beyond the stage, the sky looked Greek, like the aquamarine tint you'd see over the Parthenon as you leafed through an encyclopedia. Below that sky, so hot and yet so cool, full of every sort of promise, the golden hills and auburn woods blazed on the horizon.

"What do you want out of life?" I asked.

"Oh, I want to be a professor at a good school," she said in a dreamy voice. "I want to write books on subjects that interest me and be around accomplished people."

I realized this might be the only chance I'd ever have to be alone with Rae. I had to seize the time. I put my hands on her shoulders and massaged her back.

She let out a long breath. "What do you want to do with your life?" she asked.

"I used to think I wanted to come up here and be a star Razorback," I answered. "Now I don't know. This record thing's driving me nuts, because it's bogus. I think what I want now is to find out who I am and not be afraid of myself when I do. I don't want to hide anymore."

"That might be dangerous."

I made my life more dangerous. I turned her to me and kissed Rae. I trembled as our lips touched, and then I shook as if I had a fever.

She was startled. "Stop shaking like that," she said. Then she looked angry. I thought she might slap me. She squeezed me and let go. I could never escape being me.

"See if I ever kiss you again," she said. "It might kill you."

My pride rose. I kissed her again. She laughed and ran down the aisle of the amphitheater and onto the stage. Flinging out her arms, she launched into a recitation from *Antigone*.

I stood below on the green and applauded when she finished. Rae had taken off her mask and shown me that she, too, yearned.

Seabirds

T he next morning, I woke to an empty house. Dad had left a note saying he'd gone to Fayetteville for Homecoming and would come home tomorrow night to fix me dinner before the Squaw Hollow game.

Rae had been on my mind all night. I succumbed to dopey feelings for her. I pretended that she sat at the table and I served her tea. We didn't have a teapot, but there was an appropriate vessel. From the dusty china cabinet, untended since my mother's departure, I chose a delicate pink cup with a turquoise handle edged in silver. It contained a dead moth. The saucer was stained. Easing the moth into the trash, I tenderly washed and dried the cup and saucer. Pantomiming pouring tea, I served Rae. Her presence became real. She wore a strapless green silk dress that rustled as she moved. I admired the sweep of her shoulders, which my hands had felt only yesterday. She was medium-sized, a little wider than most girls, with sweeping curves I ached to trace. I wondered if I could ever be passionate enough for her.

I was about to become unconscious. I asked her to dance and heard the rush of her dress as she rose. I nearly fell into the sound. As my hand sought the hollow of her back, an instinctive attachment to reality saved me. I dragged myself back to the empty house. I had never mooned over a girl; now I was gaga. Maybe emotions are like childhood illnesses; the longer it takes you to catch chicken pox, the worse the case. It scared me to think how far away I had almost gotten.

I strapped on my backpack and drove to school. I signed two "Grab a Grand" badges and headed inside. Rounding a corner, I nearly collided with Rae.

"Come to my house for dinner tonight," I whispered absurdly. It was the first thing that came into my mind.

"What would *she* say?"

Missy slumped down the hall, drawn and downcast. The last time I'd seen her, she had slapped me, but now she looked whipped, and I was responsible for the beating. I guess she wanted

Michael Gaspeny

to show me the pain I had inflicted. In World Lit, everyone noticed her condition.

"Missy, are you all right?" Ms. Colwin asked.

"My sinuses are acting up."

"Shouldn't you see Nurse Andrews?"

"No, ma'am. I want to be right here."

It didn't make me proud to sit next to my victim.

In that day's discussion of *Beloved*, Rae was especially vocal, finding the patterns within patterns, as she and Ms. Colwin interviewed each other and the rest of us tried to take notes or looked out the window. I was sorry about Missy, but Rae's buoyant tone distracted me from my guilt. Only yesterday, I had been alone with her. My hands had lingered on her shoulders. We had kissed. During class, I imagined performing ridiculous acts of submission, hurling myself at her feet and thrusting my head in her lap, begging for attention. I felt her fingers working the strain from the back of my neck.

Ms. Colwin showed a video in which Toni Morrison called slavery "the American Holocaust," as horrifying as the Nazi murder of six million Jews. We saw pictures of slaves in steel collars with bits jammed into their mouths as if they were horses; of men and women whipped so often that scars covered their backs like scales; of the mutilated victims of lynchings. I wanted to scream at this evil and my powerlessness to change history or compensate for the suffering.

In addition, there was the not-so-trivial matter of my own well-being in contrast to the misery in the film. There I was in World Lit, born during the right time, with the right color and social class, exerting my privilege to mistreat one girl, worship another, and ponder a thousand-yard game. I had done nothing to deserve my fate or to lessen injustice in this world. And, while I was on the subject, how did my desire for Rae differ from a slave master's lust? Of course, I would never have forced myself on her, but the poses we struck in my fantasies were identical to a cotton king's cravings. I thought I was a sick boy and that maybe people weren't meant to move beyond their environments and should stay where they belonged, and therefore I ought to make up with Missy, no matter how much I wanted Rae, because the distance between Rae and me was too vast and impossible to cross on any level. My head spun. Stick to your kind: that was the logic the vicious creators of Jim Crow had used to maintain power.

I had the same urge to rave that had seized me after Ms. Colwin's comment about "the knight in our midst." But this time I wanted to spew a confession, to unleash the inmates in my mind.

When the bell ended class, I couldn't look at Rae or Missy or Ms. Colwin. I wanted to get drunk. I ditched school and drove to Lee's bent on getting down to business with some forties. I hadn't seen him that morning. Sometimes he only came to school in time for football practice. I banged on the garage door, but there was no music and no answer. It pissed me off. Maybe he'd gone to the hills to do what he called "Zen fishing" with a broken hook and no bait.

I got back in the car. Where could I go? Not home. The person I didn't want to be lived there. Little Walter Jacob's "Key to the Highway" blasted from the tape player, and that was where I was bound to go. Delta time! Maybe I could wash myself in the Mississippi and become a new person. I had the map of Clarksdale in my World Lit notebook.

I hit the road. Six hours and I'd be moving through zones of the blues. Daylight savings time had ended. Night fell fast. Lifted by the music, I zoomed to Little Rock and into the Arkansas Delta. I remembered I hadn't bothered to phone an excuse to Coach Chuck Hurd. I wished he'd suspend or drop me, but I knew neither would happen. His future depended on me. Imagine that.

When I left I-40 around Wheatley, traffic disappeared. Flecks of cotton glowed in the black fields, which had been recently harvested. Night thickened so that it was hard to see the faded lines on the road. I had entered a spell broken only now and then by light from a shack or farmhouse. Robert Johnson sang "Crossroads," his slide guitar vibrating between my eyes. The Mississippi River, "Old Man" of legend, wasn't far now. Somewhere out in the darkness lay the spot where myth said the Devil had tuned Robert Johnson's guitar in exchange for his soul. I wondered what Robert Johnson would think if he were around to look at me. I was always worried about the effect I had on other people. I always expected to have a relationship with them. That expectation rose from my social class and ability to lug a football. Why would Robert Johnson think twice about me? I had done nothing to deserve his notice.

I had imagined other seekers thronging to the Delta to be cleansed by the music. Maybe my fellow pilgrims were arriving by other routes or maybe they weren't coming at all. It was a Thursday night, but I'd read that juke joints were ready for business every night. I crossed the bridge at Helena, but it was too dark to see the fabled "Old Man," and my growing excitement made me concentrate on the road. I hadn't come this far to have my trip interrupted by an accident.

I hit Highway 61 and reached Clarksdale. Outside town,

Michael Gaspeny

I approached a club where a parking lot jumped with traffic, and I thought I had found the spot where the blues seekers in my imagination had gathered. But pulling off the road, I heard the chunka-chunka-chunk of rap music. The guys outside the door looked at me as if I were insane. A big sign announced the club's rules—"No guns alowd!; "No sell or use of dope on premzis!"; "No xseptions!" I got back on the road, noticing in the rear view mirror enough new cars around the club to start a dealership. I had come to Clarksdale to hear the blues, and my introduction was a hip-hop club.

I stopped in town and studied my maps by the light in the car. I decided to look for the Blue Diamond Lounge and the King Snake, two blocks away from each other. Everything was closed downtown above the Sunflower River, which looked like black molasses full of stumps. Only a rare vehicle crawled under the gaze of an old grain elevator towering over the streets. I passed two clubs on my Internet list—one closed till further notice, the other boarded up.

I pulled up to an historical marker near the railroad tracks and got out, leaving the car running. The sign commemorated the site where W.C. Handy, the father of the blues, had lived. Late at night, in a depot at Tutwiler, Mississippi, Handy had been introduced to the blues by a wanderer who slid a knife along the strings of his guitar. The sound inspired him to arrange orchestral blues. There were no traces of W.C. Handy's house, which must have been gone for a long, long time. Beyond a rusty chain-link fence lay a beaten lot that looked like a dusty passway for trucks from the warehouses beyond.

Down the street from the Handy shrine stood an old depot at the railroad tracks. The grain elevator loomed over the town like a forsaken monument, grim and reproachful. The stark town felt abandoned. The mocking vibrations of a slide guitar perfectly captured the emptiness, translating the atmosphere into sound. By comparison, the decay in the Ozarks seemed graced. Outside Spinkville, there were crumbling settlements, lost tourist cabins and souvenir stands, their cursed condition discouraging vandals. But beyond the hovels, strength shimmered in the mountain ridges and gave you a glimpse of hope. The Delta folded you into yourself, the direction I had come to escape. I had dumbly imagined a picturesque Clarksdale designed for my ease, clubs lit in pastels. I snapped at myself, "Gee, ain't it funny when the world doesn't meet your expectations?"

I rode around. Reaching the dark backstreets, I wanted to go home. Something bad had happened to the Blue Diamond

Michael Gaspeny

Lounge, which was roofed with kudzu. In search of the King Snake, I passed into a neighborhood where everything seemed to move, including the scrub-pine along the gullies in the blackness. Kids played chase or rode trikes across the bare front yards. Old folks rocked on the porches of shotgun houses. Men and women, leaning against dead cars, gestured and drank. I was the lone Caucasian in the area.

I drove with squinting, pained care, afraid a child might fly in front of my wheels. What if I hit a kid or a dog and became involved in a racial incident? I passed what I assumed was the King Snake. There was no sign, but I heard music, and in the yard, crisscrossed with vehicles, men laughed, drinking quarts of beer and watching the street. My fear edged toward hysteria. I could not imagine passing through that gauntlet—the supreme test of a courage I didn't have. Leaving the car would have been hard to do even if the men were white, but their color increased my fear. What was I doing there? My brotherly love was an empty, cringing creed. I drove by the joint three times, withered by panic.

The car crept to the other side of town. I found myself on a brick street in the black business district headed toward a dead-end. The rising wind flapped a banner in front of a club called Scales Paradise. "Welcome, Blues Lovers," the banner pro-

claimed. Except for a few cars near the bar, the street was deserted. Maybe at this place I could take my chances and recover my
pride. Maybe I could still bring something home with me from
Clarksdale. But the urge to run churned in me, too. Trying to fight
it off, I challenged myself: "You didn't come all this way to chick-
en out!"

I forced myself out of the car. The four or five customers
inside the Paradise were surprised to see me. It was as if no white
person had set foot in the bar for a long time. The music they
listened to contradicted the banner outside. A cheesy rhythm-and-
blues boy quartet sang from a boom box on the counter. This music meant I would not hear the blues there. But at least I was inside
and determined to stay awhile, no matter how much it rattled me.
Almost quivering, I took the first stool at the bar, the one closest
to the door.

"What would you like?" asked the bartender, a slender
black woman with long arms.

I ordered a Miller High Life, expecting to be carded, but
she brought me a golden bottle and a coaster without asking for
I.D. When I pulled out some money, she said, "Don't worry about
it, honey. We'll run a tab. I'm Mary."

In the friendliest voice, she asked my name and where I

was from, and when I answered, she broadcast the details to the other drinkers, who nodded and murmured politely as if my being from the Ozarks were an accomplishment.

It was not an intimidating group. A graying, handsome man in blue mechanic's overalls shot pool with a pleasant, shapely woman "built up from the ground," as the blues songs said. I heard their names, James and Ruby, as they joked back and forth. A big woman in a baggy Steelers sweatshirt drank malt liquor a few stools down from me. She ignored a short, cinnamon-colored man standing and talking in her ear. He kept saying, "Lookahere, Eunice," and then dropping his voice. Her sagging eyes were lost in the mirror behind the bar. He wore a tan zippered jacket and crisp khakis. He looked like a portrait in brown.

"What brings you to Clarksdale?" Mary asked.

"To hear some blues," I said and asked a question whose answer I already knew. "Will you have live music tonight?"

"No, but we had a big time a couple of weeks back. Look, the Persons were here." She rummaged behind the bar and handed me a poster of an extended-family band, unlikely to play the blues. "We almost tore the house down," she said.

I pretended to admire the poster. I had the feeling she was trying to prove herself to me, and that seemed odd, because I was the stranger.

Without the music, there was no reason to stay. She read my mind. "Johnny likes the blues," she announced. "We're gonna turn this tape off and play the seabird."

I knew from my reading that *seabird* was an alteration of Seeburg, manufacturer of the first juke boxes that came to the Delta. She took some quarters from the cash box and led me to the dim back of the bar. The juke box hadn't been played in a long time. The dusty floor preserved our footprints.

The warm laughter from the pool table touched me. James and Ruby pleased each other. I was not used to adult couples having fun. My father and mother had torn each other apart. In Spinkville, rich or poor, husbands and wives planned, worked, and prayed together, but they did not play. They measured their lives by home improvements and church projects. Strange how easily Missy and I had fallen into step. Away from the crowd, we were skittish, and it wasn't only because we were young. I couldn't imagine us delighting each other over a game of pool. I wondered if we had ever shared a natural laugh. I admired the warmth of James and Ruby.

Mary fed some of the bar's quarters to the seabird and encouraged me to choose songs. All my idols were there—Muddy Waters, Howlin' Wolf, the three Kings (B.B., Freddie, Albert), Robert Nighthawk—and so many more whose names I knew but whose records I had never heard—J.B. Hutto, Hound Dog Taylor, Earl Hooker. I savored my selections, while Mary returned to the bar. The music washed over me; I unwound a little.

The pool game ended. James said he had to go to work, and his goodbye wave included me. The man in the tan clothes, the composition in brown, walked to the back. Keeping a wide distance between him and me, he entered the doorless men's room. As the records changed, I heard him snorting what I assumed was cocaine. He came out, staying even farther from me than he had before, and returned to Eunice, who wore the Steelers' black and gold. He resumed talking, but she paid him no mind. Ruby tidied up around the pool table, putting cues in the stand and dumping the ashtray.

I went back to my stool. Mary put another beer in front of me, saying, "I can tell you really like that music."

"It means a lot to me. Do you like it?"

"I like newer sounds. But, you know, we get people from all over the world coming to blues country."

She was trying hard to be hospitable, but I couldn't fight off my suspicion.

Ruby sat down next to Eunice and ordered a Champale. Before long, they were laughing. The man in the tan jacket resented the intrusion. He went to the men's room again and strutted back, hovering between the women. Their hands talked along with their voices, flapping, poking, touching each other's shoulders. It was fun to watch the women enjoying themselves. Their faces fascinated me: Eunice looked bewildered, as if the answer to a problem fluttered just beyond her; Ruby's tender expression was a picture of understanding.

The short man said, "Know what I think when women get close like these two?" No one answered, and he replied to himself, looking at me. "One wants the other's man or else they want to play nasty with each other. Which you think it is?"

"Hush up, Walter," Ruby said in the brightest way.

"Well?" he said to me. When I hesitated, he said, "I'm waiting."

"I don't think it's a good question," I answered.

"Say, hey! Our young, yodeling cracker from the mountains finds my question out of line, but God doesn't. He says it's on the main line."

Mary interrupted. "According to the song, Jesus is on the main line, and you ain't the son of God."

"I'm a child of God and I'm ordained."

Mary said, "Ordained in cocaine! You preached in that piddly church of yours, and the flock fled."

"Maybe you like what they're doing."

"What are they doing?"

"Maybe you want to join in."

"That's all! Nobody should have to listen to your shit. Get the hell out of here," Mary shouted.

"So you can mix with this mountain oyster?"

"Out!" Mary yelled and tore from behind the bar, shaking a billyclub. Walter jerked the club loose and raised it to hit her. I grabbed his arm and twisted the club free. It rattled across the concrete floor.

He seemed to fall apart. "Keep your white hands off me!" he screamed, looking sick. "Are you crazy? You don't have any idea what's in my pocket. What the hell are you doing here?"

He left, cursing and shaking.

On the seabird, Freddie King did "Someday, After Awhile (You'll Be Sorry)." His mellow guitar phrases soothed me.

Mary said, "I feel bad that had to happen in front of you."

"It's all right."

Ruby said, "Walter's lonely and crazy and had too much

toot."

Eunice slowly shook her head, saying, "He ain't happy unless he makes everybody unhappy."

"Mary, you better call the *po*-lice if he comes through that door again tonight," Ruby warned.

Eunice added, "Yeah, and he always comes back, sometimes with those gangsta cousins of his from L.A. They use the Delta like a hideout."

"Like we're living in the Wild West, girl," Mary said. "You okay? I am so sorry you had to get mixed up in Walter's mess."

I wanted to tell her that I wasn't royalty, that I could take care of myself, but I said, "I'm fine. No need to apologize."

"Let's pretend this never happened. Play us the blues," Mary said and gave me some quarters. She was spoiling me like a child.

As I stood at the seabird, the poisoned look on Walter's face returned to me. He hadn't just been furious because I wrenched the club from him. My touch had made him ill. The man had looked contaminated. It was amazing to think skin had such power. It gave me a small sense of how black people must have felt when whites acted as if their skin was disgusting.

Michael Gaspeny

When I went back to my beer, Ruby finished her Champale. "I have reached my limit," she announced, wished us good night, and left. Mary accompanied her to the door and watched her drive away. Eunice had the last of her malt liquor, said goodbye, and dragged herself out the door, barely raising her feet. Mary ducked outside and watched her go.

With Ruby and Eunice gone, the Paradise got bigger. I was about to leave, too. I had a partial victory. At least I had tried to find the blues.

Mary returned to the cash box and counted the little money there. "Not much business tonight," she said. "I'm closing up."

"Owning a bar must be a lot of headaches," I said.

She laughed. "Oh, honey, I don't own this place. I just work here. In the daytime, I clean."

I started to ask where, but I realized it was probably for people like me.

She pressed her long fingers together. "Listen, I know a joint where they might have some blues tonight. The real deal. I want you to get the best of Clarksdale. What do you say?"

"Sure," I replied and put a twenty dollar bill on the counter.

"On the house. You kept us all out of a fight."

"But that's not right. You shouldn't lose money on a customer."

"I do what I do," she said and stuffed the bill in my letter jacket pocket. "Let's go."

I started for the door, but she brushed past me and told me to wait. She stepped outside, ducked in, hesitated, and repeated her surveillance. "Crackheads all around here. Might as well be Chicago," she said.

She locked up, and we got in my car. She kept checking the street as I pulled away from the curb. Her concern seemed exaggerated until I remembered she had been just as careful when Ruby and Eunice left.

She guided me far away from town. Her clothes carried a scent of floor wax and cleansers. It reminded me of hopeful times, the first day back at school and the promise of the season-opening kick-off. But I realized what lifted my heart probably caused hers to sink.

Now that we were out of the bar and alone together on a dark road, I searched and searched for something to say. As often happened when I strained to break a silence, I asked a dumb question. "Do you clean at home after you clean all day at work?"

"Oh, my place is neat, very neat. Would you like to see?"

"Maybe later."

I wasn't attracted to Mary, and I hoped I wasn't encouraging her, and yet maybe I was.

Out of the flat, dark nowhere, I saw cars scattered in front of a cinder-block building canopied with vines. Some of the vehicles looked as if they still ran, while others formed a maze of wrecks. When I pulled off the road, I heard the music. Jagged notes shot from the juke and spread over the fields.

Inside the club, Mary shouted to the woman behind the bar, "Tonya, this is Johnny. He come a long way to hear the blues."

Tonya had thick, rolling shoulders. Mary gave her some cash. I couldn't understand Mary's crazy generosity. Why couldn't she let me pay for anything? She didn't have any money. She was a cleaning woman moonlighting in a beer joint. Was it a matter of pride or Delta hospitality, desperation or desire? Maybe they were parts of the same damn thing.

There were about twenty people drinking from whiskey bottles and quarts of beer and shaking to the music. A wide, bullet-headed man in a sweaty green nylon shirt sat in a chair and played guitar. Two young guys, all bones, accompanied on bass and drums. No one sang. Sometimes the wide man moaned or yelled. The band raised an extended howl with a pounding beat and eerie, rasping notes that crawled all over me—deep blues that struck me between the eyes and in the spine. I raised my arms and swayed. Mary looked surprised. The force of the music swept me away. My life in Spinkville receded like a town I had whipped past on the highway. I was filled with gratitude.

I began to move with no idea where I was going. There seemed to be no end to my exhilaration. It gusted inside me, jerking me along, sending me spinning and twisting. My bones shook as if they wanted to fly from my skin. I ached so fiercely that I moaned, and then I was beyond the pain. My fit shocked Mary. I guess she had seen plenty of out-of-whack white people before but no one like me. My body was behind me now, leaving nothing but feeling. It seemed I had lived my whole life for this moment. From the first time I heard a slide guitar, this was my destination. Until I reached the juke, I had only glimpsed how much I wanted to escape myself.

Mary held my waist, but I flew away from her. She tried to stay between me and the other dancers. They had been conditioned to be patient with Caucasians, but they were smoldering. The crowd tolerated me as long as I behaved, but I had no control over myself. The more the music seized me, the more I wanted. I grew wilder and wilder. When I beat my fists against the wall, Tonya helped Mary push me outside. Her eyes sparked at Mary.

Michael Gaspeny

She told us to never come back. Out in the yard, I threw my shoulders against the ruined cars as if they were blocking sleds. The wrecks shook like tin. Mary yelled and yelled. Lovers' arms and legs churned in the windows, and people bellowed. A man with a knife jumped out and warned us away. It was a miracle he didn't stick me. Then, driven by the music, I circled the club, slamming myself against the cinder block building.

Mary tried to drag me to the car. Just as she pulled me into the maze of wrecks, two men struck me, and I hit the ground. A flashlight blinded me, and a familiar voice said, "Now, boy, we're gonna hear you yodel."

"What us do with this white trash?" one of Walter's guys asked.

"Yeah!" his friend said.

They probably came from the hip-hop haven I saw on the way to town.

"Stand him up!" Walter commanded.

I tried to resist, but the fit had spent me, and I was a disembodied impulse. They jerked me up and caught me in a chokehold.

My eyes were scorched. Mary kept cussing and shouting, "Let go of me!"

Walter said, "You like white men so much you're going to give him a souvenir."

He tried to hand her something that she wouldn't take. "Bitch," he said. "You best do as I say or I'm gonna turn these young gentlemen loose on you. They don't like race-mixing. Cut him, you hear me? Start right there."

I couldn't see where he was pointing, but it made me frantic.

"Damn me, damn you!" Mary howled. "I don't know why I brought you out here."

She seemed to explode. A blast of cleaning agents burst into my nose as she slashed my face. Then she was off and running. A wet streak stung from my forehead to my chin.

"Now you are a postcard from the Delta," Walter proclaimed.

His friends pounded me, and I was out.

Michael Gaspeny

My Debt to Society

The next time I opened my eyes, I was heaped in the mud on a foggy morning. Two crows rocked and inspected me. When I moved, they flapped away. Fighting off dizziness, I stood, staggered, and collapsed. The gash pounded. There were pulsing knots on my head and a knob on my spine where Walter's guys had kicked me. They had turned my pockets inside out. I crawled to a willow tree, rose in stages, and supported myself until my head settled and I had my balance. The fog cleared. I dragged toward the light and stopped. I stood on a bluff overlooking the gray Mississippi. The river lay to the east. Somehow I was back in Arkansas.

I looked hard at the water, but there wasn't much to see. I

had read in an earth science book that below the lazy surface, the Mississippi was lashed by such violent tentacles of current that you couldn't plant your feet on the bottom. If you got tackled by the ankles, you drowned. In my shame and stupidity, I considered offering myself to the whirlpool. My toes flexed as if I were testing a diving board, but the desire to jump subsided. I turned and stumbled to the road. The car was gone.

I walked along the levee for awhile until I saw warehouses in the distance and made out *Helena* on one of the blistered walls. My most immediate worry was how in the world I could explain my blood-stained, broken-down condition once I reached town. I wobbled like a chewed-up dog. I had to will myself to brace my shoulders and walk straight. Even then, I kept veering. I could have been mistaken for a drunk. What if a cop stopped me and asked what the hell I was doing?

The riverfront in Helena was a forlorn collection of abandoned buildings, stores struggling to capitalize on the city's blues heritage, and hole-in-the-wall bars. Throughout the area, you could see where renovations had begun and petered out, charting the tide of money and hope. The only folks out that early were a pair of derelicts scouting aluminum cans, which they dropped in a filthy white plastic garbage bag. They looked at me without surprise. They had probably seen plenty of bedraggled boys with sliced faces. Maybe I belonged to their group.

The hospital was a long walk from the river. I kept following signs, but I didn't seem to get any closer. A hard sun came out. This was November, I had to remind myself, but Helena seemed stuck in August, with heat waves rising from the asphalt in dusty neighborhoods of scorched-looking houses. I walked the scarred blocks, where dogs nosed trash, no one was going to work, and I was just more damage. Everyone was friendly. A black man standing at a corner waved and waved at my approach. I waved back, said good morning, and asked if the hospital was around here, but he couldn't speak, and his expression never changed. When I looked back, he was still waving. The sun struck his face, and he looked overjoyed that I had passed his way. That man was as wired to repeat himself as a traffic signal. I waved a last time.

I reached highway 49. There, last night, I had been a seeker on wheels pondering the ghost of Robert Johnson. Now I was a vagrant with an infected face approaching a tourist center. The enthusiastic white woman behind the counter didn't balk at my appearance. She welcomed me to Helena and directed me to the hospital, a turn down the road. As I left, she gave me some pamphlets, including one about the blues, and urged me to visit the Civil War sites. Outside the tourist center, I felt like crying because she seemed to see the sky beyond the scars—a hopeful attitude. That was probably an illusion. If my life consisted of one false notion after another, this one, at least, didn't seem dangerous.

By the time I reached the emergency room, my feelings were swollen by confusion and self-pity. The receptionist seemed like the sister of the woman at the tourist center. Without my wallet, I couldn't prove my identity and show an insurance card, but it didn't matter. She asked if I'd been the victim of a crime.

I said, "I got drunk and passed out on a bed of glass."

"You ought to be more careful about your accommodations," she replied. "Anymore in Helena, we have drive-bys."

A soppy mood came over me while I waited for the doctor. I remembered James Cotton, Muddy Waters' harmonica player, called Helena the meanest town he knew. I wondered why the city had to seem so abandoned, why there had to be drive-bys anywhere, least of all in a small river town, and why anybody had to be afflicted like the waving man on the road. Nothing was fair. Sick of myself, I was also sick of everyone who could be implicated in the fate of the Delta—God and politicians and Mr. and Mrs. John Q. Citizen. I remembered Mr. F, in a rare somber mood, called life a fast fall and said you had to protect yourself as best you could. Reflecting on growing up in Drumlin, he claimed there was a food chain in society just as there was in nature and that an honest documentary about a town would have a lot in common with a show about the jungle on Discovery Channel. That had sounded harsh to me, but at the time I had thrived at the top of the food chain. Now I bore the marks of his wisdom.

How the hell would I get home? If I hitchhiked with a bandaged face, I'd look hideous, a fugitive from an asylum. Who would pick me up? I didn't know where Dad was staying in Fayetteville. I wasn't eager to inform him about my trip, the lost car, and the cutting. My pathetic condition would come close to breaking him. I thought he deserved a few more hours of peace. I knew Mr. F would disapprove of my fool's vacation, but he was experienced when it came to trouble. The nurse let me use the phone. I called him at Intercontinental, told him I'd been in a scrape, and asked him to wire money for bus fare, food, and the emergency room bill. He insisted on coming to get me. I couldn't talk him out of it, so I told him to pick me up at the visitors' center on highway 49. I had five or six hours on my hands.

When the nurse took my temperature, I had a fever. The doctor said it was too late to sew up my face. He cleaned up the gash and applied some bandages to draw the sides together.

"Besides falling on glass, how else do you entertain your-self?" he asked.

"Play football."

"Son, your season's over."

I didn't know if I was happy or sad. The nurse gave me a vial of antibiotics and a few extra-strength Tylenol in an envelope. My head burned. I felt a little crazy. I thanked the doctor and nurse and said it had been great to be in Helena. Walking back to the visitors' center, I sat at a picnic table under willow trees. There was no business. The welcome woman brought out two Cokes. She had a thin smile, hive-like hair, and a name-tag that said "June." While the pills took effect, we discussed music, especially native son Sonny Boy Williamson, the great harmonica player, and his legendary radio show *King Biscuit Time*. It beamed from Helena all over the Delta. You name a mighty bluesman from the '40s and he appeared on the show with Sonny Boy—Robert Nighthawk, Robert Jr. Lockwood, Elmore James, Muddy Waters, Howlin' Wolf, scores more. In blues history, Helena had been a fabled city.

"This place should be a shrine," I said, mounting my high horse. "But do you think you'd ever find the name in an American history book or hear a teacher mention it? What if I told people,

Michael Gaspeny

'Every time a rock song moves you, you're indebted to Helena, Arkansas and Clarksdale, Mississippi'? They'd call me crazy. Think about the cover records. Most people believe Led Zeppelin created 'You Need Love' instead of Willie Dixon and Muddy Waters, and the Rolling Stones wrote 'Love In Vain,' not Robert Johnson."

June gave me some advice: "Don't take it so hard. Don't be too hard on others. Just spread the word. Remember there was a time when you didn't know, either. The words to blues songs all have roots in the beginning. In most cases, nobody knows who made up the lyrics. Sometimes the person getting credit was just singing what he heard at fish fries when he was a kid."

"You know more than I do," I said.

You never reached the bottom of the blues. Like Sonny Boy in "Eyesight to the Blind," somebody in Africa had probably sung a tribute to a woman whose shining beauty drove a blind man to see.

Fatigue hit me. My head eased to the table, and I fell into a dream. In a dark bar, I approached a lighted juke box. I pressed a button. A record started to play. Suddenly the disc screeched, and it came alive, bursting into birds that shot by my head. The birds had faces I recognized—Mary and Rae; Missy and Walter; Lee

Branch; the women at Scales Paradise; Coach Chuck Hurd; even Billie Holiday and Muddy Waters. They whirled past the pool tables and cue rack, swept over the stools, behind the counter, and by the plate glass window, raising a racket, tearing at one another. I couldn't tell whether they were after blood or love. Was it both? Then they banked like pigeons and whizzed back into the warm machine.

I watched the record spin and tried to hear the music when a voice called me out of the dream. Mr. F stood there in a charcoal suit and a pearl-gray tie.

"Johnny, what happened to your face?" he asked.

"I got cut."

"You had to see for yourself, huh?"

"Yes, sir, but I couldn't bring it off."

"Let's pay your bill at the hospital and get you home."

I waved goodbye to June in the visitors' center and directed Mr. F to the hospital. When we entered, his elegant clothes caught people's attention. He looked like a VIP, what Ms. Colwin would call "a dignitary." I sensed folks thinking, "Who is that man?" Except for their Sunday best, I knew fashion wasn't first among the folks in Helena. The staff moved quickly, especially when he brought out the money clip.

In the immaculate Lincoln, we rolled through cotton country toward the interstate. Flocks of red-winged blackbirds perched on wires over the linty fields. They flitted back and forth across the highway, the yellow borders on their red shoulder patches glowing. It was hard to feel hopeless in the presence of such stunning birds and Mr. F at the wheel.

"What are those birds doing here?" I asked. "They can't eat cotton."

"Beats me. If I were a bird, I'd be somewhere else."

"I know this sounds crazy, especially to see what I look like today, but there's something about this place I like."

"Sometimes folks like the places where they had the most excitement, even when it was bad news," Mr. F said. He had a way of pointing you toward a conclusion without hauling you all the way there. He wasn't happy with my attitude.

I told him the whole story. At the end, I said, "For awhile at the juke, when I first heard the music it was so beautiful," I said. "But I ran wild. I really screwed up."

"You paid for it."

"It's not that simple."

"You ought to make it that simple. You have to forgive yourself. You aren't born knowing everything."

"Some people know more than others."

At that moment, Mr. F's aura meant more to me than his advice. He radiated pride. He was comfortable with himself. He didn't get in his own way. Until further notice, I was the opposite. For some time, maybe for the rest of my life, my idiocy in Clarksdale would haunt me. I had begun to serve a sentence of self-disgust. In my solitude, I would make myself ill by leafing through the album of my stupidity in Mississippi. In my daily life, random impressions would return and leave me cringing.

In Russellville, we stopped to eat at a place known for its buffet, but Mr. F insisted on ordering different items. He didn't want what the public ate. I recalled his visit to the Golden Gate Bridge. When he held the cable, saw the land end, and gazed at the Pacific, maybe he grasped the possibility that everything could be better. I could see that faith in his deliberate manner with even the smallest things. He was present in his own life. He had a subtle, sacramental way of acting. When he paid the check with bills from the money clip, he looked like a magician. His presence gave me a little lift. Lost in my thoughts, I reached the door, when I noticed he wasn't with me. I looked back. He was tottering among the customers at the steam table. Terrified, I rushed to him. His right kneecap was twisted, bulging outward like a knob inside his

Michael Gaspeny

charcoal trousers. I had seen this happen before to a kid during a basketball game in gym class. The kid fell and screamed at me, "Put it back!" which I forced myself to do. Now Mr. F grabbed my arm as I slid the cap back into place. Groaning, he hesitated and then took a few trial steps until he found his stride.

"My knee," he said. "Sometimes it slips out. Sorry."

"It's all right," I answered. Thank God he was okay. The sight of him lame and wobbly shook me up.

"Let me drive," I said.

"No, no. I'm fine now. I just never know when that's going to happen."

On the road, I thought about how much pain he'd absorbed to discover his style. I hoped one day I could reach a similar grace. You didn't get there without pain. That was my first positive thought in a long time.

I asked, "Do you think much about your days on the scout team and taking those night walks?"

"My knee likes to remind me now and then. But mostly I follow Satchel Paige's saying: 'Don't look back; something might be gaining on you.'"

Maybe some day I, too, could fix my eyes on what was in front of me and outdistance my old self. But just now it was a football Friday in Spinkville, and, for the first time in four years, the hope of the town would not take the field.

When Mr. F pulled into my driveway, I said, "I don't know how to thank you."

"I do," he replied. "Don't beat yourself up."

He knew I wouldn't do what he asked. As I left the car, he shook his head.

While he drove away, Dad rushed from the porch. "What happened to your face?" he asked. "Are you all right? Where have you been?"

"Mississippi," I said, hurrying by him into the house.

"You have scared the hell out of me. Coach Hurd's losing his mind. The whole town's looking for you."

"So was I."

"Where's the car?"

"Stolen."

Dad tried to swallow his temper, but I wished he'd explode and get it over with. "Are you ready to play ball?"

"No, sir. There's a long gash under this bandage."

"What!"

His Spinkville Purple Dog paraphernalia lay ready on the kitchen table—pennant, seat cushion, umbrella. I imagined him

Michael Gaspeny

running his fingers over these sacred possessions as he waited for me.

"I'm sorry," I said. "I didn't want to worry you. I planned to be back before now. I made a mistake. I meant to call you."

That last statement was a lie. I had only thought about calling him. Once I reached Mr. F, I forgot all about Dad. At the least, I could have phoned from the restaurant in Russellville. Dad would have been back from Fayetteville by then. But, as Mr. F drove me home, Dad had never come into my mind, except for the pain I was bringing him, and for that I felt sorry.

I tried to tell him what happened, steadying myself by holding the chair where I had lately imagined Rae sitting. But my story became a summary, not the living thing. I had spared nothing in my account to Mr. F.

"We can deal with this later," Dad said. "It's time to get to the game."

"I told you I can't play."

"Then you need to support the team."

"I don't care about the team right now."

Dad jittered around the kitchen as if he'd drunk four cups of coffee. He opened and closed drawers, silverware chiming. "What in the world were you doing down there?" he asked.

"I wanted to hear some music."

Shock had turned his face gray as granite. It was horrible to see him like that.

"How could you jeopardize an undefeated season?" he asked, raising his voice—a rarity. "What are the recruiters going to think? You can't hide something like this. Music! I never thought I'd be a parent to say this, but you need to stay away from that music. It's eating you up! It's all about backdoor men and mean, mistreating women. It celebrates recklessness and self-destruction."

"No, it reveals what's deep inside you. Don't blame the blues. I did it all on my own."

"You're protecting the damn music like it's your girlfriend!" he shouted.

I nearly yelled, "Maybe it's my mother," just to hurt him, but I didn't.

It was almost time for the kick-off. Dad pleaded with me to go to the game, but I refused.

"Well, then, one of us has to be there," he said. He had duties. After all, he was president of the Booster Club. He gathered his Purple Dog paraphernalia and hurried out of the house.

His desire to keep up appearances pissed me off. After

what I saw and did in Clarksdale, Dad's preoccupation with football seemed ridiculous. All the years we had watched games together were gone. Once, not so long ago, Dad's devotion to his Purple Dog souvenirs had amused me. Now I scorned the image of a grown man shaking his Bulldog key ring for good luck during the kick-off and waving a pennant whenever Spinkville made a first down.

I wanted to get drunk, but I didn't want to be seen. Lee's Golden Lounge was the perfect spot. He was on the field; the door was always open, the refrigerator stocked with golden Miller High Life. With my car gone, dumped perhaps in a Delta swamp, I felt a twinge of nostalgia as I hid myself under a hooded sweatshirt and walked out to the highway. Across town, the stadium lights glowed, and drums rattled and rolled. Lee lugged the ball for me. Except for clerks in stores, everyone was at the game. I had the road just about to myself. As the season passed and the victories mounted, the crowds had grown, swelling the stands on both sides of the field, the bleachers in both end zones, and circling the fence separating the track from the field. All those fans were speculating about me, and, right then, I didn't give spit about any of them.

The lounge was lit. I let myself in and went to the refrigerator. I took a pair of forties, which along with the pills I had left from Helena, would ease my night. I uncapped a forty and took a long pull. God, it was good. A negligee lay on the wrestling mat a few feet from the bathroom door. It seemed to be looking at me. I thought I was hallucinating. But drawing closer, I saw that there were eyes on the fabric. Tweety Bird watched me! It was strange to see a canary on such an enticing garment. I wondered whose flesh throbbed below the negligee, and the image began to have its way with me. I decided to play a sympathetic tune before I left. Selecting *Johnny Hartman and John Coltrane* from Lee's LP collection, I went to the turntable to play "Lush Life," a state I wanted to reach. The record player was warm. Lee had been gone for at least two hours. Coach Chuck Hurd made us report to the locker room by five-thirty; Lee always came in a little later. Someone had been playing records a short while ago. I realized the owner of the gown hid behind the closed bathroom door. Maybe she and Lee had done some warm-ups.

Listening to "Lush Life" and guzzling beer, I began to feel loose, even criminal. A mixture of pain, sorrow, and mystery pulsed in me. I resented Lee and his preaching. I wanted to rip off the bathroom door and take the treasure inside. My feet squeaked on the mat as I approached the door. I began to sing along with Johnny Hartman, but my voice was cold. The girl heard my brutality. She must have been holding her breath, because when she started to cry, the sobs tore out of her and unmanned me. The lock clicked on the bathroom door.

"Tell Lee Johnny borrowed some beer," I called and walked home shaking.

By the time Dad got back, I had taken a pill, passed deep into the second forty, and reached the bottom of a golden ocean. Dad's agitation was as distant as waves breaking far above me. He paced the living room like a frantic coach on the sidelines. He said we were going to a meeting with Coach Chuck Hurd in the morning. The Purple Dogs had beaten Squaw Valley to remain undefeated, with Lee saving the day by scoring two touchdowns in the fourth quarter. Lee would keep on scoring all night, I thought. Dad had actually said, "We beat Squaw Valley." I wanted to mock him by asking if he'd made any tackles, but I was so out of it I slumped to my room and drifted away, listening to Robert Johnson and drawing Rae close to me.

In the morning, I didn't hear Dad till the door flew open. "I've knocked enough," he said. "Get up!"

Hurting everywhere, I stuffed my pounding self into my clothes. When Dad and I reached school, workers applied the last licks of purple paint to the brand-new press box. The wind carried the pungent odor of the paint, and it almost gagged me. In the coach's office, the usual bucket of chicken livers and carp chum was gone along with Coach Chuck's quid of Red Man. With all the attention attracted by the thousand-yard game, maybe he had cleaned up his act. I knew that spiffy image would fly like the last leaves as soon as pigskin season ended. Principal MacMartin, whose scalp glowed through his fading flat-top, waited along with a stranger who had a drooping moustache. Coach Chuck introduced him as "Doc Coombs." His jowls reminded me of the fat around a pork chop.

The principal informed me that I was suspended from school for three days as punishment for skipping yesterday. I almost laughed because the sentence allowed leeway for me to practice Thursday and take the field against Esmeraldo the next night. MacMartin cleared out, leaving matters to the coach, who suspended me from the squad for the same length of time and then said, "Doc's gonna take a look at that cut."

I noticed the squat, unhealthy-looking man had been called "Doc," not "Doctor." I imagined him chomping a cigar in the backroom of a bar and dealing cards from a marked deck. Easing the exterior bandage off my cheek, he peeled off the interior dressing. His squinched-up, glinting brown gaze almost hypnotized me. He had some kind of mojo. His fingers moved like a breeze. He barely seemed to touch me. He might as well have wished the bandages to leave my skin. Dad gasped while Coach Chuck appraised the wound.

"Oh, Johnny, what a terrible thing they did to you," Dad said.

"My fault," I replied. "I might as well have done it myself."

"How'd you get that, son?" Doc Coombs asked.

"Cut outside a juke joint."

"How come nobody sewed you up?"

"My treatment was delayed."

"Good thing you weren't permanently delayed."

"I'm not so sure about that," I said.

My so-called physician chuckled. "You've got a live one here, Chuck," he said. "Boy's got tone."

"He ain't cracked a joke his whole career," Coach Chuck Hurd said. "Then, all of a sudden, he's playing the fool down in fever country. Can you speed the healing process, Doc?"

"Sure thing. It'll be browning up in two days if he sticks to my regimen."

In the movies, at least, most doctors carry their implements in a shiny leather bag, but this porky man with the supernatural touch kept an assortment of curiosities in a wooden, barn-shaped box. He tilted my head back and stirred a swab in a plastic jug that looked like it contained cough syrup.

"Just a minute there," Dad interrupted. "What is that gunk?"

"Home brew," Doc said. "Gonna sting like the dickens, Johnny."

As he applied the raisin-colored concoction, my cheek flamed, and I almost shot out of the chair. He brushed the cut three more times, and each layer felt like he took a cigarette lighter to my face. It was a wonder my cheek wasn't crackling and smoking.

When he was satisfied, my eyes were stinging. He passed the jug to my father, saying, "Now, Dad, see this stuff's applied every four hours, four licks at a time. Change the dressing, but don't wash anything. Don't use anything else. Just keep painting it on."

He dressed the wound, gave Dad a box of gauze and bandages, and left. He was short-legged man, but he moved like a blur.

Coach Chuck swayed back in his chair, his fingers twined behind his head, his gut pillowing out. He looked like he was carrying a child; the sight made me nauseous. He tapped a stack of papers on his desk. "Thirty requests for press credentials," he said, "and they're still rolling in. Can you believe it?"

Swallowing the bile in my throat, I said, "Those people are going to be disappointed. The doctor in Helena, who was a real doctor, told me my season was over."

The coach chuckled, smiled, and shook his head. "You know what it says about Doc Coombs in the New Testament, Johnny?"

"What are you talking about?" I asked.

"It says Doc brought Lazarus back to life and told him to play dead till Jesus came." He laughed and looked me in the eye. "You'll be toting the ball, Hoss. Everybody's future depends on it."

He opened the door and smiled us out of the office. As we left, Lee waited for his Saturday morning meeting with the coach.

"What happened, Man?" he asked. "All kinds of rumors are flying around." He put his hands on my shoulders. It had been years since he had shown such concern for me. I was touched.

"It's a long, long story. I'll tell you later."

Dad, who was behind me, heard what I told Lee. Out in the car, Dad said, "I think you better keep this story to yourself."

"I've already told Mr. Futrelle."

"It's safe with him. He's a good man."

I wanted to say, "Better than good," but I didn't.

At home, I went to my room and listened to Howlin' Wolf. Dad interrupted and asked me to come to his study. I dragged myself in there and stood with my back to him, looking out the bay window at Spinkville spread below us. From our house on the hill, you could see the best part of town, which looked like a village in a model train exhibit. Oh, we had tracks, but no train had come our way for at least ten years. Saturday morning vehicles shined as traffic flowed down Main Street and eased around courthouse square.

"I have to ask you an honest question," Dad said. "You didn't have unprotected sex with that barmaid, did you?"

Tension had roused a lord-high tone in him. Mr. Futrelle was "a good man"; Mary was "that barmaid."

"No, sir. Her name's Mary. She was nice to me, and I was a danger to her. I was the problem down there."

Pacing in front of the window, he seemed to be building a legal case. "You know a person isn't automatically good because she's black or bad because he's white, don't you? Is it possible you like black people a tad too much?"

Michael Gaspeny

I wished there was a forty in the house. "I don't know many black people," I said. "But I do like most of the ones I know."

"There are more black people in Spinkville than you ever realized."

"What do you mean?"

"Black people in white face. They worked at the plant and enabled us to live like the pharaohs of the Ozarks."

"Were they singing, 'Tell old Pharaoh, let my people go?'"

"No! They were uncomplaining. They always took the hits. But I got tired of people losing fingers chopping chicken and going crazy on assembly lines so your mother and I could get drunk and pitch scenes in New Orleans."

"So you sold the plant."

"Yes, but it didn't make me popular. Folks around here like tradition, and they hate corporations. They'd rather have a boss they know in rehab than a new suit as a CEO. When Intercontinental came in, they felt sold out. For a few years, they stayed cool to me no matter how I tried to help the town. Then, in middle school, you started scoring touchdowns, and people thawed. We hired Coach Hurd, and you became a star for the Purple Dogs, and the two of you helped me get elected mayor. Did you know that? In this town, football is Friday night church!"

He thumped the desk and almost struck the family Bible. I wanted to laugh.

"So you're saying I should break the record for the sake of my Father in heaven, my father on earth, and our many black residents in white face?"

He pounded the desk with his fist, and this time the Bible shook. "How about for your own sake? You could honor those lost fingers and also make yourself a hero."

"I didn't ask for anybody's finger. And that record's a lie. How in the world does it help people to feed their illusions?"

He cleared his throat for a counter-argument, but he couldn't find one. I had stumped him. I went back to my room and Howlin' Wolf.

I spent the days of my suspension trying to get my head right. After Clarksdale, I loved the blues more than ever. I took heart from the voices of my idols as they, speaking for all haunted people, insisted on their superiority to pain and disaster. Hounded by my delirium in the Delta, I tried to keep that message close. I thought about Mary and the trouble I had brought her and how the next time a white person walked under the banner outside Scales Paradise, she ought to close the bar. But I knew she wouldn't. I imagined her serving a beer, saying, "We'll run a tab," and presenting the seabird to the next pilgrim. She had the decency that comes from trusting yourself, something I lacked.

On Monday, Dad and Coach Chuck announced that I was improving, but my status for the Esmeraldo game remained questionable. When, the next day a few reporters called to cancel their credentials, the coach upgraded my condition to probable.

That night, when Dad came home, he said, "The whole town's asking about you. It's amazing how concerned people are."

I wanted to roar. Instead I asked, "Concerned about me or themselves?"

"Maybe they don't see the difference. That's the definition of the home crowd."

On Wednesday morning, I sat in my room, listening to Buddy Guy, when Dad came to the door. "There's someone here to see you," he called and left the house.

Missy stood in doorway. She started talking, but I couldn't hear her.

"What?"

"Turn the music down."

I clicked off Buddy Guy. We went to the breakfast room.

"I would have come sooner," she said, "but with all the preparations for the Esmeraldo game, there's no time. There's never been anything like this in the history of Spinkville."

"That tells us where we live," I said. My snotty tone reminded me of Rae's, and I cringed.

"How do you feel?" Missy asked.

"I'm starting to heal up."

It had been only a short time since I'd seen her, but the morning of the video in World Lit seemed as if it had happened in another life. If she had looked broken then, now Missy was a ghost. I felt like holding her, but that was the result of my weakness—an attempt at the easy way out. I guess only a sadist enjoys the sight of his victim.

"It's time for us to break up," I said.

"Yep," she said. "I brought your stuff in the car. Six years of ancient history. My room is just about bare."

We went to the driveway. Three clear plastic bags of memorabilia were packed in the trunk of her car. A teddy bear I had won at the county fair looked disgusted with me. She jerked the bags from the trunk and slung the souvenirs at my feet.

The ghost turned red. "You better get your butt to that

game tomorrow night," Missy said. "If I can cheer the way I feel, you can play with a cut." I started to speak. "Don't interrupt me. Don't talk to me anymore! Don't you *ever* say another word to me!"

She got in the car and drove away. I threw the mementos in the garbage can. I admired the way Missy acted. She had more character than I did.

I wondered if I ever loved her, whatever that word meant. I had played my part with her for so long that it seemed natural. I had never thought about my acting until I listened to the blues. Would I have stuck to my stage self if Rae had never come to town? Did I love Rae? I thought so. My desire wasn't momentary. The flame didn't waver. She suited an ideal form that existed deep inside me—a pressing shape. Of course, I could have been wearing rainbow-tinted shades. That so-called ideal, that pressing shape, could have been plain old desire or straight-out lust. Recent experience had taught me that if a human consisted mostly of water, then illusion filled the rest. I'm misguided; therefore, I exist.

The Road to Glory

Missy left about noon. A little later, I was surprised to find Lee at the door. It had been years since his last visit. The temperature was in the forties, but he was bare-chested, the field of hair jacketing his trunk. He carried two forties in a sack.

"Aren't you cold?" I asked.

"Aren't you hot?" he answered.

For the first time that fall, Dad had turned on the heat. The dinging radiators released a smell of iron, dust, and flaking paint.

Lee said, "Let's drink some beer and pitch some shoes."

Our Olympiads of long ago often concluded with horse-shoes ringing at dusk.

"I'll see if I can find the shoes."

Michael Gaspeny

We went to the backyard and the old, neglected garage with swollen sides and a sagging roof. I had not been out there in a long time. When I opened the door, the past overwhelmed me—a reek of sweat-dyed football gear, grass stains, gasoline, and dusty, cracked vinyl on old glider cushions. The horseshoes rusted on hooks attached to the wall. I wiped them off with an old rag dipped in gas. I took several long whiffs of gasoline, a smell I loved; it had the odor of raw manhood. I should have kept a gas can in my locker to jack me up before games.

Behind the garage, the pits were grassed over, but we took things as we found them. We were out of practice; our tosses did more rolling than sliding. Lee asked me about the Delta, and I talked. My story absorbed him more than anything I had ever told him.

"How alive did you feel?"

"Counting fear?"

Lee nodded.

"Tops." I realized when I was around Lee, I sometimes sounded like him.

"I'm impressed."

"There's nothing to be impressed about," I said. "I went down there, and I couldn't take it."

"You faced things, Man. You didn't hide."

"A lot of things worry me about it, like what I got Mary into."

"She's an adult. She probably wanted to jump your bones. But don't forget: She cut you good."

"She didn't want to do it."

For awhile, I was glad to have Lee's company, but it was no fun to pitch shoes. Some simple rites can't be recaptured and should just be left alone, casualties of time. We had lost our feel for horseshoes and were only going through the motions. The old security of the game was gone.

We went behind some bushes to retrieve a couple of shoes.

"Listen," Lee said. "There's something I want to tell you: Rae and I are seeing each other."

"What?"

"Yeah, it started last Thursday when we ran into each other at Grab 'N' Go."

"You're not kidding?"

"We're seeing each other for real."

I started cussing.

"It just happened. It was before school. We were getting

Michael Gaspeny

drinks at the same time. I was actually going to school that day. That obese bastard Bob behind the counter was giving me shit about violating the 'No shirt, No service!' sign. I hadn't thought about it. I apologized, but Bob wouldn't shut up. It was embarrassing. I wasn't trying to be an asshole like I sometimes am. I mean I was blushing. And Rae said, 'Aren't you a friend of Johnny Spink's?'"

I felt like bashing Lee with a horseshoe. "Spare me the details!" I yelled.

"We kept talking in the parking lot, see, and I gave you a big build-up. I didn't have any designs. Luella Lang has been keeping me busy. Rae talked until it was past time for school. We went for a ride. One thing led to another. She was, like, ready. She's human, Man; she's a girl. She likes thin-crust pizza and Tweety cartoons. She was there the other night when you got the beer."

"I saw her Tweety gown on the floor. Fucker! While I was getting cut, you were living my fantasies!"

Lee took a long pull from his forty. "I'm not apologizing. What happens, happens. I dared you to call her. Remember that night at the garage when I put the phone in your hand?"

I started to tell him about the amphitheater, but those two

kisses seemed pathetic, even laughable now, especially the first one.

He said, "If you couldn't call her then, don't complain to me now."

He finished his forty as he walked off and flipped the dead soldier in the trash barrel behind the garage, his self-satisfaction unshakable.

I was in a mood to get wrecked, but there was no more Lee's Golden Lounge. What was left of me? Missy was gone, as she should have been. Rae was "mating" with Lee. I couldn't exactly call Mr. F for advice. I didn't care what was happening at school or anywhere else in the world. Now I was nothing but my music and my cut. I went into the house and removed the bandages. Yep, that gash was deep and jagged, but it wasn't infected anymore. It looked less angry than forlorn, like a thick brownish-purple lace dangling from a shoe in a dumpster. Doc Coombs' healing panacea worked wonders. In the old days, he could have sold that potion in a traveling medicine show. I swabbed the wound four times, my face flaming. Like pain so often did, it struck the nape of my neck, jerking me awake. If I wasn't a blues pilgrim or a lover, I was a football player. I called Coach Chuck Hurd and told him I couldn't wait to play.

Michael Gaspeny

"I knew it all along," he said. "You got a hunter's heart, Johnny-boy."

Talk about absurdity! I was a hunter, all right—a self-hunter. I had almost hunted myself into the ground.

I had to see Rae. In the morning, I set off for school early, backpack slung over my shoulder, hoping to catch her at the Grab 'N' Go. Its orange sign glowed a quarter of a mile down the hill from my porch. How often had I seen it on my way out the door and never even thought she could be down there with the commoners? Oh, how I had glorified her! I entered the store, poured coffee, and tried to pay Big Bob. "On the house," he said for the first time ever. I roosted at the igloo-shaped Swirly machine and read *The Mountain Eagle*. Tate Donner had written a piece about a bet between two evangelical ministers in Spinkville and Esmeraldo over whether I'd gain a thousand yards. The loser had to host a pig-picking with all the fixings. Coach Chuck Hurd had spread the news that I was going to play. The Grab 'N' Go customers were happy to see me.

About a quarter to eight, Rae came in, looking hung-over after a night of wrestling at Lee's Lounge. She was dying for a Swirly. She didn't notice me until she put a king-size cup under the dispenser of the machine and pressed the button.

"Johnny, you look terrible!" she said.

"You don't look so vibrant yourself."

"Dad told me what happened. Do you need a ride to school?"

"Yes."

Behind the counter, Bob got an eyeful. She paid for the drink, and we entered her Kelly green Taurus. It was as neat as her father's Continental, not even a speck of dust on the dashboard.

"How do you keep your car showroom-clean?" I asked.

"I don't let it get dirty."

"Then you must have the feet of an angel."

She drove one-handed and sucked on the straw of the Swirly as if the drink were life support. Passion had drained her. In blues songs, love was often described as striking like a storm that shook your bones and rattled your teeth. It must have been ecstasy to join with her and make thunder and lightning.

Instead of a storm, a sweet plea rose from the tape-deck. The breathy Supremes sang "Someday We'll Be Together" from a Motown's Greatest Hits compilation.

I said, "I thought you only listened to gospel or classical music. You told me that once."

"You could call this 'inspirational.' It's based on an old

spiritual," she said and slurped the drink. "Lee said he told you about us. That's the way he is. Existential. He's big on facing things."

"Especially when it's the other person who has to do the facing. Hey, remember when you and I went to the amphitheater?"

"I was in a funny mood that day. I'm sorry if you got the wrong impression."

She pulled into the parking lot at the stadium. Purple and white crepe paper flapped from the goal posts. The band was practicing, instruments gleaming in the sun. The new press box glowed.

The sight of the field, where I had so often worked my will, stirred me. I said, "I wonder if we could recapture that funny mood."

"I don't think so. You're not such a bad guy, Johnny, but we don't click. It's the girl who's supposed to tremble."

I could have beaten my head against the shiny dashboard. I had never clicked with anyone in the way that she meant. Maybe Missy and I came close the day we skipped school, but desperation had fueled us.

When we left the Taurus, ninth and tenth graders gathered like sheep between us and the school. Rae finished the drink as we made our slow progress, kids high-fiving me. She dumped the empty cup in the receptacle as we entered the building.

"I need something for my head," she said and went to the water fountain.

I stopped under the stairs and watched her take some pills. I realized how rarely I had looked directly at her; most of the time, I had seen her from the side. Standing there was a pathetic thing to do. Her most trivial gesture interested me, and that was a big part of my problem. You don't win a girl by worshiping her. But how do you stop?

It was a long school day. I had not kept up with my assignments; I didn't know what was going on. I slouched in my seat like the biggest slacker at the school. Teachers left me alone, some because I was not to be disturbed during this momentous week, others because I was scandal-stained. At practice, a non-contact Thursday, all we did was run through plays. Some guys resented my absence last week, but I was beyond caring about their feelings or the needs of the team.

As I left the locker room, Tate Donner asked if I wanted a ride home. He had curly hair and the Schlitz waist of an old-school sportswriter. His appearance was an asset to his trade: it had a relaxing effect and made people talkative. He was treasured for his encyclopedic knowledge of Arkansas sports and his witty, accurate stories. I preferred his nostalgic streak to the cynicism I had noted in other sportswriters.

We got into his dingy white car, the interior littered with press guides, sports magazines, and stat sheets. When we closed the doors, the pages fluttered. The engine coughed a few times as we rode away from school.

"How are you holding up?" Tate asked.

"I'm sick of the whole thing."

"It'll be over soon."

"I don't know if it'll ever be over," I said.

His sputtering vehicle was almost over, trailing smoke all over town. The engine needed an emergency overhaul.

"Tate, I think this car is falling apart. What kind is it?"

"A Comet," he said. "Some people call it a 'Vomit.' I'll take it to the shop soon."

"You better do that sooner than soon."

You could smell the smoke inside the car, but all that ever concerned him was the alpha and omega of sports. Tate said, "Most people support you a hundred percent, but some are grumbling that you've gotten too wild and turned your back on the town."

"I wish I knew how to be wild. Don't those people ever have problems?"

"It's because they have problems that they're so interested in the record. You take their minds off their problems."

"So I'm entertainment?"

"In Spinkville, you're Mr. Show Biz."

Tate drove aimlessly. The Vomit crept east away from the mountains. It was the road I had taken at the start of my trip to the Delta only a week before. At the Dairy Dream, we pulled over for a snack. In middle school, after our team won an away game, the bus stopped here for a treat. I was always alert after a game, almost supernaturally so, and I saw things in fine detail. I loved standing in line on the dusty shoulder of the Dream, which was just a hut with picnic tables outside. Under the lights, dirt looked blond, and bits of glass glittered in the ground. Lemonade and fruit punch swirled in plastic containers, and you could smell chili in the sharp air. The hits from the game trilled in my bones.

The "then's" and "now's" of my life didn't connect. Except for my name, I didn't feel like the same person. Tate and I took our food to a table and ate in the cold. I opened up to him. He asked if this was on the record. I said I didn't care. I told him all about Clarksdale, including Walter's horror at touching my skin and Mary's generosity. I guess one of the reasons Walter made Mary use the knife was to avoid all contact with me. He acted as though white skin were diseased. I wondered if he threw away his shoes after kicking me. I was lucky to be alive, but then a corpse can't remember or serve as a postcard.

When I got home, Dad paced the front yard. He grabbed a rusty rake just as the headlights hit him and tried to look busy. Tate wished me luck, and I left the car. I could tell Dad was fussing around out there because he was afraid I had run off again. I had become the kind of shaky person others were forced to worry about, perhaps like my mother.

I ducked past Dad, went to my room, and picked up *Beloved* with the idea of improving my understanding of what Ms. Colwin referred to as "the author's devices." Then I realized that even if I became the world's foremost expert on Toni Morrison, Rae would never have wanted me as I did her. Fed up with myself, I fell asleep listening to Billie Holiday singing "God Bless the Child." She had been cursed by an impoverished childhood, predatory men, and heroin addiction, but her one-of-a-kind voice turned pain into beauty. I took heart from her, hoping I could overcome the mess I had made.

I woke up ready for Esmeraldo. It was bright, cold, and

clear—great weather for a running back. I vowed to set the record if I had to carry the whole town on my back for a thousand yards. On the breakfast table, the paper lay open to Tate's column, which I read as Dad served eggs, bacon, grits, and biscuits. Something always got lost when another person told your story, but Tate's piece was an accurate account, with a few discreet omissions. I was grateful to see the truth in print.

"Is that what you told Tate?" Dad asked.

"Yep!"

"You're trying hard to face things, Johnny. I admire that."

It was interesting that for different reasons Lee Branch and Dad expressed the same opinion. Lee liked danger. Maybe Dad was learning that he and I had separate lives. Until a week ago, I had been a model son. It was easy for Dad to think our relationship would always be like it was on those old autumn Saturdays in Fayetteville. Our disagreement about the record and my trip to Clarksdale forced him to see later than most fathers that he and his son did not walk the road of life side by side.

"How's the cut?" Dad asked.

"A thick, raisin-colored scab."

"I'm taking you to a plastic surgeon next week."

"No way. However it turns out is what I look like. It's

me."

That morning, Dad exceeded his high level of care. He poured more orange juice, gave me twenty dollars, and offered me a ride to school, which I declined.

I loaded my Walkman and set off on foot. As I wound down the hill and into town, there were graven images of number 11 everywhere. I decorated lawns like a homemade saint. I struck a stiff-arming Heisman Trophy pose atop the spinning sign of Farmers National Bank. There were placards in windows, messages on marquees. Every business ran a promotion involving a thousand something or other.

Rae's Taurus was parked at Grab 'N' Go. I wondered if big Bob was selling thousand-ounce Swirlys. When I passed there, folks stepped outside and shouted encouragement, including Bob himself, who rarely shifted from behind the counter. I saw Rae's profile, but she didn't turn around. I waved at the people giving me the good word. Moving through town, I had the stupid fantasy that Rae, suddenly recognizing how much she loved me, came running and caught me in her arms.

The Pope hadn't come to Spinkville nor had a crew from *Sports Illustrated*, but the city was packed with media from all over the state. I was so good for the local economy that I thought about petitioning the Chamber of Commerce for a slice of the profits. Diners were jammed; at Ed's Exxon, TV vehicles dwarfed the pumps. Horns sounded like distant crows' cries beyond Muddy Waters singing "You Can't Lose What You Ain't Never Had." The song was three minutes of truth—the title the perfect comment on human vanity; every feat would be topped; every achievement would suck exhaust and eat dust. You didn't own anything or anybody. Muddy knew the score about unrequited love: Rae had never been mine anywhere but in my fantasies, and yet I felt forsaken. The song also said that no matter how much we whined, we caused most of our problems. Muddy's tone conveyed both sadness and biting humor. It said now that you've been a fool, it's time to stop wallowing in self-pity and find your feet.

At school, teachers keyed their lessons to the theme of one thousand. Spanish and French translations of "Grab a grand" were posted on classroom doors. A history teacher lectured on what North America was like in 1000 A.D. A business teacher, focusing on the power of the great millennial number, brought a thousand dollar bill to class and passed it around; all day, kids swooned over touching that bill.

Ms. Colwin used the occasion to discuss "The Battle of Maldon," commemorating carnage in 991. I didn't give a rotten fig about anyone else's limbs on this day. I sagged in my desk and disconnected my mind, that is, until Ms. Colwin's discourse led to epics and she mentioned the magnificence of such literature in other cultures and the lack of an American epic. Some scholars said works about the settling of the West were our great epic, although they were composed by multiple authors. Others called *Leaves of Grass* an epic of the nation's soul.

The wires in my head hummed. Suddenly I said, "As I understand your definition, an epic requires a larger-than-life hero who overcomes great challenges while covering vast territory. The story must be told with dignity, and it should involve supernatural forces."

"That's most of it," the teacher said.

"Could a resilient people rather than an individual be the hero?"

"I'm not sure about that."

My mind was flying, and my tongue chased it: "Is the Old Testament of the Bible an epic? It's not focused on one specific hero, but it tells the story of a tribe's struggle for survival, and it contains supernatural forces."

My question caught Ms. Colwin off-guard. Her response started in one direction and skittered in another. She reminded me of a ball carrier who can't find an opening. Finally, she said, "Let me think about it. I'll give you an answer Monday."

I had an agenda to pursue no matter what. "What about a story that begins with a people stolen from their native land and oppressed in the New World? What if the folk react by inventing an art form that expresses tragic struggle and contains such truth that it becomes a metaphor for the human condition?"

My classmates gave me puzzled looks. I sounded professorial, and I didn't care. I wanted to appeal to Ms. Colwin in her language.

"What are you talking about, Johnny?"

"The Blues!"

"But the Blues relate the experience of a minority."

"In the Bible, the Jews are a minority, aren't they? They had oppressors. The Jews get enslaved just like black people did. We all know it's still going on. But keeping on point, white people are present in early blues songs, whether they're named or not."

Rae interrupted me. She wanted to bail out the teacher. "I think he means spirituals and gospel songs."

"It's all the Blues," I countered. "The music of deliverance. One of the reasons Robert Johnson sinks to his knees and begs for mercy at the crossroads is because of the position white people have put him in. He says everybody drove by him. How many black people owned cars in the Mississippi Delta? Robert Johnson couldn't have been who he was without the bigotry of whites. Let me play the song for you. It's in my backpack."

Oh, Ms. Colwin was vexed. "We don't have time today," she said.

"This is important. Couldn't we make time?"

"I'm sorry," Ms. Colwin said, "but we can't transform injustice in one class period, which is what you want to do."

"Why don't we make a start? I just took a little trip to Mississippi, as you may know from the newspaper..."

I was about to rave my way into a public confession roaring far beyond Tate's account when there was a knock on the door, and Ms. Colwin escaped to the hall.

She stuck her head back into the room and said, "Johnny, Coach Hurd wants you. Take your backpack. Good luck tonight."

It may have been the first time any teacher was glad to see Coach Chuck. He usually came seeking passing grades for floundering players. As I left the room, I wondered if she had somehow pressed a button summoning him, but that was absurd.

"What is it?" I demanded of the coach. "I was making a point!"

"Damn, you're getting feisty. Save it for the game. Come

with me. We have an appointment to keep."

He led me outside where the athletic van, emblazoned with purple canines, waited. He drove us to the regional hospital. I assumed that a licensed physician, not Doc Coombs, would make a last examination of my cut. But my assumptions were always wrong. Coach Chuck took me to the children's wing, saying, "I want you to meet someone."

He entered a room, smiling and waving, and I followed. The sandy-haired boy in bed sat up so fast that he shook the I.V. attached to his right wrist. A suture curved from his cheek to his neck. It was hard to look at.

"This is Justin Wiggins," the coach said. "He's had some growths removed from his jaw, so he can't talk just yet. He wanted to meet you."

Spotting Justin's "Grab a Grand" badge, I grasped the purpose of the visit. Coach Chuck took an alphabet stencil from the bedside table and put it in Justin's hands.

The coach said to me: "You can ask Justin questions, and he'll answer by pointing to the letters. He's real quick that way."

I lightly shook Justin's left hand and gave it a soft press. "How are you?" I asked.

He pointed to the letters, "I, O, K."

Michael Gaspeny

"See?" the coach said. "Justin's right handy. He's one of your biggest fans. His grandfather worked for your folks for forty years, and just about every one of his relatives has been connected with the plant one time or another. You could call it 'a family tradition of service.'"

I had to congratulate Coach Chuck on his bedside manner. Justin beamed.

"Justin wanted to give you something, Johnny."

The boy's left hand moved to a tablet on the night-stand. With the coach's assistance, Justin removed a drawing and handed it to me. It showed number 11 floating down field with a stiff arm ready to dump a tackler.

"Justin saw your touchdown run against Fort Kean on TV, and he's done a crackerjack job of capturing it, if you ask me."

At the bottom of the picture, Justin had written, "Deccated to Johnny, Justin," which I took to be "dedicated." The drawing must have been hard to do under the circumstances.

"Hey, this is good," I said. "Can I sign your badge?"

His eyebrows wriggled, so I applied my most careful signature. I hoped the badge wouldn't disappoint him tomorrow.

Coach Chuck said, "Justin, is there anything else Johnny can do for you?"

I knew the answer. The stencil didn't need numbers. Justin pointed to an 'I' and three 'O's.'"

"I can't promise you the record," I said. "Strange things happen in a football game. I'll try as hard as I can. But there's one thing I can promise: When you get better and play on a team, I'll come to see you play." I wrote my phone number on the badge. "You call and tell me when, okay?"

The boy's brows and fingers flexed. I thought about telling Justin that one day we might compare scars, but I snuffed that idea. When the coach and I shook his hand and started to go, Justin motioned for us to stop and then spelled out "thanks" on the stencil.

In the hall, Coach Chuck said, "Now that was mighty touching, wasn't it?" although he was the one smiling and I had the misty eyes. "You don't want to let that little feller down, Johnny."

The coach was right. He had concocted an airtight script. His hypocrisy was so out front that I wanted to laugh and howl in disbelief. He represented the opposite of everything I respected, but I couldn't hate the man. He was too ridiculous.

When we returned to school, it was lunch time. In the parking lot, Lee and Rae lounged in the front seat of his VW van,

Michael Gaspeny

sharing a cigarette.

"Look at that," Coach Chuck said. "He's teaching her to smoke. One's going to the paratroopers, the other to the Ivy League, and ain't a soul gonna mess with either one of 'em. Why, they could do it in the road, Johnny."

We flashed past the smoking lesson, but Rae stuck in my head like a slide.

At the pep rally that afternoon, I entered the stadium to the roar of "John-*ny*! John-*ny*!" As hard as it must have been, Missy did an inspired job of cheering. I admired her resilience. It would be good for both of us when this year ended. People often said senior year in high school was the best time of their lives, but I wouldn't be one of them—and neither would she.

After school, I walked home past the thick traffic. Kids shifted into a party mood, hanging out of car windows and joking with me. Their antics provided a pleasant distraction. Once I climbed the hill and closed the door of the empty house, I got scared. My pre-game ritual was to chill out and listen to music, but I could find no peace. I kept whipping around in bed. It was as if there were two Johnny Spinks—the real me, who seemed independent of my family and town, and the second Johnny, who belonged to others. The real me wanted nothing to do with that bogus thousand-yard game. The second me had obligations to Dad and the past and Justin Wiggins. That second self occupied a position of ease in the world bought by the sacrifices of citizens below the hill. How would I have liked to gut turkeys forty hours a week to enrich other people? Maybe I had no right to do what I wanted; maybe I had to act on behalf of others. For a different reason, Mr. F approved of my grabbing a grand. He told me not to reject a gift because in this life, you need all the gifts you can get.

The game had so consumed my thoughts that I hadn't wondered what I would do afterward. My life had become tonight. By the final whistle, my highlight reel would end. I had lived seventeen fairly routine years to reach an eight-day stretch where I lost my mind in a juke joint; came to the end with a girl I didn't love; and got ditched by the girl I did love, who was riding my best friend, who treated me like the new boy in a Zen monastery, where the sensei lashed a cane across my shoulders to raise my awareness.

Gloom took me. I did not think things would improve after the game. It might be corny, but it was true that you couldn't like the world, if you weren't happy with yourself. And I did not like myself. While I was on the subject, how could I have dared to hope that Rae would like me if I didn't? My thoughts were so bleak

I felt like battering down walls. I wanted to play football now. Bring on the Esmeraldo Rebels! The night I had dreaded for months now offered me more comfort than anything else in my life.

Dad came home, broiled my pre-game steak, and called me to the table. I forced myself to eat, tore into the meal, and finished fast.

Throwing down my napkin, I said, "Dad, give me a ride to the game." It was the first time I had spoken the word "Dad" in quite awhile.

"Isn't it early?"

"Please, I want to go now."

I grabbed my Walkman. I had prepared a special tape of favorites—Blind Lemon Jefferson's "Match Box Blues"; Mississippi John Hurt's "Frankie"; Muddy's "You Can't Lose What You Ain't Never Had" and "My Home Is in the Delta"; Howlin' Wolf's "Smokestack Lightning"—the first blues song I ever heard—and "Goin' Down Slow"; two versions of "Angel of Mercy" by Albert King and Albert Collins; Freddie King's "Goin' Down"; Robert Nighthawk's "Goin' Down to Eli's"; Buddy Guy's "The Things I Used To Do" and lots of Billie Holiday. I wished I could have a tape blazing inside my helmet, a slide guitar shrieking in my brains and guts, driving me to batter Esmeraldo.

It was almost dark as we got in the car and wound down the hill. My illuminated image spun on top of Farmers' National Bank. I wanted to climb up there like King Kong and pulverize it. I was overloaded with testosterone. I felt vicious. I wanted to hit now. It was too early to feel so "cock-strong," as folks said back in the hills. I didn't want to burn myself out by the kick-off. Concentrating on "Angel of Mercy," I tried to talk myself down.

Driving through town was slow going. Normally the streets were deserted at this time, but pumped-up kids cruised with engines revving; cars throbbed with head-banging music; beer cans clattered across parking lots. Beyond my sweet music, horns blared as people spotted our car. This season had given me a micro-dose of celebrity, and I never wanted to taste that drug again. It would blow you apart. I didn't know how anybody could stand it. For the first time, I sympathized with movie stars and ballplayers with mega-million dollar contracts. I was determined to live the rest of my life in anonymity.

It was a relief when we finally parked in front of the gym. When we got out of the car, Dad hugged me and asked, "Is there anything I can do for you?"

"No, sir," I said. "It's all up to me."

My Last Dash

My Walkman and I were about to enter the locker room when a red-haired man with skin as slick and shiny as a mushroom stepped outside. He identified himself as a reporter from Little Rock and opened a small notebook.

"What are you listening to?" he asked.

"Blind Lemon Jefferson."

"What kind of music do they play?"

"It's a man, not a band. A great old-time Texas bluesman."

"What does that music do for you?"

His tone irked me. "No comment."

"Then tell me what it's like to be black."

"What do you mean?"

"You said in Tate Donner's column that you knew what it's like to be black."

"No. I said I had a small sense of what black people had to experience because down in the Delta my white skin made a black man hate me."

"Then are you a wigger?"

"What's that?"

Back then, I had never heard that word.

"A white person who imitates blacks."

I had already said too much to a fool. "I've got a game to play," I said.

"That may be so, but this business won't go away."

I hurried into the locker room. I had never been so glad to see Coach Chuck Hurd. Instead of the usual, "Here comes The Man, the stud-horse!" he asked how I felt.

"I want to play right now. I want to hit!"

My ferocity surprised him. I acted like he usually did. "Why don't you go back in my office?" he said. "Kick back. Listen to your sounds."

I entered his sanctuary and zoned out. Doc Coombs came in, jerking me from the mercy of Mississippi John Hurt's loving voice.

"Hey, boy! Let's have a look at my handiwork. Stayed out of jukes this week?"

"Yes, sir."

"You don't sound happy about it," he said, peeling my bandages with his breeze-like touch. "I don't believe you've learned the error of your ways."

"Maybe not, but the lesson sure made a mark on me." I laughed at my little joke.

"You're an amusing guy, Johnny."

"Not really."

He chuckled and applied some pink stuff that drew the sides of the cut together like magic glue. He stood back and appraised his work. Satisfied, he dressed my cheek in stronger bandages.

"That ought to do it. A few minutes ago, I told your Dad to get you a plastic surgeon."

"I don't want one. This is the real me."

He pretended to study the bandage, but actually he examined me. "Watch out, Johnny," he warned. "Don't fall in love with learning the hard way. That's when the laughs end."

I had a feeling he had walked that walk. Then he vanished. I think I heard the door close. It seemed a wonder that I had heard his voice. I guessed he had done a lot of running. Whatever his troubles, that man did supernatural work. The left side of my face looked like a package you could ship to hell.

The trainer taped my ankles as I tried to pay attention to the coaches' chalk-talk. Everyone except Lee watched the coaches. He sat on the bench and stared into his locker—the way he always prepared himself. Instead of hanging his clothes on hooks, he had neatly folded and stacked them on top of his sandals at the bottom of his locker. That way, he could empty his mind into the darkness. I wondered if he was shedding images of Rae. If so, I wished I could collect them. That's how gaga over her I was. "Hey, Lee," I imagined saying. "I'll take what you throw away."

Coach Chuck Hurd kept his pep-talk low-key—no shouting and pad-pounding. He said we had the rare opportunity to make history. When we succeeded, as he knew we would, we would have a proud memory to take with us everywhere on the highways and byways of our lives. No one could take it away from us; no one could tarnish it. Then he reminded us of the folks who had worked themselves to the bone so we could be playing tonight. He spoke of farmers scratching at the rocky ground and folks sweating and aching at the poultry plant to put us where we

Michael Gaspeny

were today. Now was the time to show our gratitude to our kin, our friends, and our hometown.

We yelled and slammed one another's pads. The assistant coaches threw the doors open, and we charged onto the field like bulls. There was a special surprise on the track behind our bench—an electronic tote board visible to both sides of the field ready to provide an up-to-the-second tabulation of my yardage.

How vengeful I would have felt if I had seen that sign from the other bench! It was a demeaning, in-your-face disgrace, but I had to remember that this game was an artificial event from the get-go, and therefore none of its parts could be handled with dignity. The tote board froze my raging blood. Suddenly stiff and tired, I dragged to the center of the field for the coin toss. We won, and, of course, elected to receive.

I slumped back to the bench while the band played "Johnny B. Goode," the overflow crowd shook signs and rattled cowbells, and the cheerleaders, led by Missy, arrayed in new spangled skirts, spun cartwheels. The greater the fever, the slower I felt. I was crashing under the hoopla. I thought if this travesty was what it took to get people excited, then Spinkville was a feeble place and I was the town's top baboon. Why didn't I take the first handoff and race out of the stadium and into the future? But that was wishful thinking. I had tried to run out of my skin in Clarksdale and look what it got me. I yearned to be anywhere except inside my mind.

Coach Chuck kept me off the field for the kick-off. He risked me on kicks only when we were desperate. Besides, return yardage didn't count toward the record. We ran the ball back to our 40. On the first play from scrimmage, I took the hand-off and slanted off tackle, but my legs felt dead, and the outside linebacker gave me such a good lick that I was about to pay him a compliment. That is, until he yelled in my ear-hole, "There, Nigger-lover!"

I recognized his voice as belonging to one of the Esmeraldans who had promised to burn me a new one in Fayetteville. The comment restored the spring in my legs and gave me a cause. I had lost a yard. In the huddle, I demanded to run the same play. This time I ripped into the hole, flattened that bastard, and gained forty-five yards before six Rebs hemmed me in and yanked me down. I heard the insult once again while a claw tore at my bandage. They were a terrified bunch. They had no confidence that they could avert the record, so they started with last resorts.

Robotic tacklers kept repeating the taunt. The guys who talked trash to me on Dickson Street had told their teammates

Michael Gaspeny

about Rae. By most standards, I had an incredible first quarter, gaining 152 yards, according to the tote board—an astronomical, absurd figure. But if you multiplied that number by four quarters, the result still fell pitifully short of the mark. The zeal of the crowd had dimmed a little. The fans saw how hard I was running, and yet I had barely made a dent in the fabled thousand.

Some of the Rebels had the marble eyes of assassins. They looked drugged-up. Under optimum conditions for them, in the dark, away from the field, a few of those boys, skinhead material, could have clubbed or stabbed me. I warned myself to watch my back after the game. Those guys were longstanding victims of abuse. In four years of existence, they hadn't won a game. They were the butt of community scorn and the laughing-stock of the Ozarks. Being on that team must have been like living with a rash that grew more infected by the season.

Football was the one thing that everybody in the hills knew. When you played, folks didn't let you forget it—for better or worse. Now, the hype surrounding this game had called the state's attention to Esmeraldo's impotence. The end of last year's game gnawed at them. With us winning 60-0 and seven seconds on the clock, Coach Chuck Hurd, following his scorched soul policy, called a double reverse in an attempt to increase the slaughter.

In ninety-nine cases out of a hundred, coaches ordered quarterbacks to take a knee in that situation. After the game, Hal Halleck, the Rebel coach, took a poke at Coach Chuck, and a cop had to separate them.

By the last play of the first half, I had a bunch of touchdowns. I tried to avoid the tote board because I didn't need more pressure. Running straight up the gut, I gained about thirty yards, carrying three Esmeraldans with me. While I was on the turf, one of the tacklers jumped up and kicked me in the helmet like it was a pigskin. My habit was never to show pain, to bound up from the pile no matter how hard I had been hit. That reflex dragged me to my knees, but no farther. My central nervous system was disconnected. Unable to stand or fall, I felt embarrassed. Penalty flags fluttered to the field. The crowd was enraged. Coach Chuck and the trainers quizzed me on how many fingers they held up and what my name was. I answered with perfect clarity, but my body was stuck. They flipped me on a stretcher and swept me off the field. The tote board caught my eye: 453.

In the locker room, the sensation slowly returned to my body while our team physician Dr. Wardle used a pen light to examine my pupils and otherwise fussed around me. I straightened my legs, stretched my arms. My limbs were restored, but I did not ever want to feel stricken like that again. Doc Coombs watched from the entrance to the shower. While Dr. Wardle and Coach Chuck Hurd consulted, I ate an orange and felt better.

"Can you go?" the coach asked. It seemed funny, as if he were asking a machine to turn back on.

"I wouldn't miss it."

I wasn't being sarcastic. I wanted to be responsible for my own fate. I couldn't let a kick in the head settle the issue. Doc Coombs buttonholed Coach Chuck at the edge of the showers, and they snapped at each other. Doc's face turned the pink of a German Johnson tomato. Coach Chuck said something. Then Doc did his disappearing trick with one sudden glare at me, his whole face pantomiming the word "No!"

Then Reverend Turley, our spiritual adviser, came in to give us a prayer. He asked God to provide us with the strength to do the best we could, and we all knew what that meant—the record. He urged us to tell God the things we wanted, but I couldn't believe if God cared, He would do anything but rebuke the sleazy proceedings in Spinkville on this night. What I really wanted after the game was Rae in my arms. God was about as likely to send me Rae in her negligee as he was to answer Reverend Turley's transparent prayers.

When we tore out of the locker room for the second half, the crowd raised a great cry, the likes of which I hope never to hear again. It came from the gut, and it contained as much pleading as encouragement. The cry was meant to remind me of my duty, to lift me up and drive me on, but whether the fans realized it or not, it also expressed their own desperation. It seemed to say, "Don't leave us to ourselves." The force of the crowd's need pressed against my back.

The Rebels could think of no new strategy except to increase the slurs and dirty play. I guess proof of being stuck in hell is repeating futile gestures. Their panicked stupidity infuriated me. I wanted to grind this ignorance under my cleats. Every insult, gouge, and late hit drove me harder. My inspiration struck our fans, whose cheering grew louder, crashing like waves, as I battered Esmeraldo and the tote board flickered. In the first half, Coach Chuck had called a token hand-off or two to Lee, but now I was the offense. Lee's blocking reached maximum brutality. His crumpled victims groaned as I flew through the hole. He was destroying those kids. At the start of the fourth quarter, I had eight hundred yards and about twelve touchdowns, and I was feeling stronger and stronger.

Esmeraldo resorted to a new low in strategy. To run time

Michael Gaspeny

off the clock and keep the ball out of my hands, Hal Halleck made his quarterback take the snap, retreat, and dance around for as long as he could without stepping out of bounds, which would have stopped the clock. Halleck didn't care how badly his team lost as long as I didn't gain a thousand yards. This trick reduced my opportunities for yardage because it left us close to the Esmeraldo goal line.

Spectators pressed against the low fence next to the track behind our bench, jeering and shaking fists. All of Halleck's tricks were craven, but this one violated the nature of the game—a humiliating, play-to-lose ruse. I doubt if anyone in the history of football had ever resorted to such warped strategy. Cowardice arouses aggression. My will and Coach Chuck Hurd's fused: I wanted to crush Halleck and Esmeraldo.

Coach Hurd counterattacked. When the Rebels gave us the ball on their 11, he had our quarterback race in the wrong direction way back in our territory and take a knee. The disgusted referees called time-out and chewed out both coaches, who got up in the refs' faces and returned fire. With all the back and forth, I hadn't noticed the tote board for awhile. When play resumed, my yardage stood at 915, and we had the ball on our ten. By getting to the Rebels' end zone, I could grab the sacred grand. There was another possibility: I could walk off the field. The night had become a fiasco on top of a mockery. Two teams vied to lose ground in this perversion of football. But quitting would have increased the chaos and left me alone with my rage. Contact was the only option.

All I had to do was run the field one more time to gain my freedom. I wanted to see the tote board flash four figures. Then I would throw my helmet up in the air and dash from the stadium. I could no longer separate the game of football from its manipulation. No amount of pressure could force me to play one more game. For the first time ever, Spinkville would enter the playoffs in pursuit of the 4-D state championship, with its stud-horse staying home.

All night one of the big holes had been off right tackle, where I had heard the first slur. Several times, I had veered through the gap, cut upfield, and run against the grain, using the momentum of would-be tacklers against them. They couldn't stop fast enough when I shot past, and, in their frustration, they couldn't de-program themselves. Because the pickings were easy, I had fallen into a predictable pattern. Now it occurred to me to fake a cutback, surge outside, and streak upfield along the sideline. If I could outrace the secondary that would be the last run I

Michael Gaspeny

would ever have to make.

I called the play myself. Lee led the way, leaving a linebacker in a fetal position. I hit the hole clean, cut inside three steps, and felt defenders shift weight to catch me as I moved against traffic. Then I changed directions, cut upfield along the sideline, and sprinted faster than I had ever run. I was free at the fifty, beyond the skidding safety man, the markers flashing by, no one within twenty yards.

Around the 10, something struck me high and low and whirled me out of bounds. It was two Esmeraldo fans in motorcycle gear who ran to their machines and roared away, Confederate flags on their black leather jackets flaring. I wanted to rip the riders off their bikes, but they were long gone. The smoke from their flight hung in the end zone as penalty flags flew, the crowd bellowed, and the refs held a frantic consultation. Coach Chuck Hurd ran screaming down the opposite sideline. The tote board read 995, intimidating the refs as they talked technicalities. They, too, had a stake in this ludicrous piece of history. They didn't want to be associated with a tainted record. Each time they were about to break from the pack, one of them raised a qualm. Noise from the crowd dimmed. Nothing deflates a stadium like a drawn-out parley by the zebras. The fans had lost spirit. Exhausted, they wanted to go home. The Esmeraldo bus pulled onto the track.

At long last, the refs penalized the Rebels half the distance to the goal line, placed the ball between the 5 and 6 and blew the whistle for the game to resume. The time had come to vault over a 1000. Coach Chuck Hurd called his favorite play, "Blast Left," in which Lee and the entire line pulled to form a flying convoy leading me around end. As we broke from the huddle, the cheers from the stands sounded thin and ragged. The long delay had exposed the citizens of Spinkville to the absurdity of a game in which two fool coaches schemed to surrender yardage. It may have forced the fans to incriminate themselves. They were fatigued, maybe even embarrassed. As the center crouched over the ball, Esmeraldo called a time-out. Hal Halleck waved his players onto the bus. There were only about thirty Rebels, and they moved fast. Esmeraldo chose to forfeit rather than grant me the thousand. There were boos, but no rage, except for the fury from Coach Chuck and our assistants. By then, most folks were leaving. Tomorrow would not be a day of civic pride. Across town, soul-searching would accompany the removal of the decorations. After awhile, everyone would forget the night's discomfort. I would be the one left with the game.

I felt shaky as we wandered off the field. A few drunks

made war-cries about the playoffs, but there was no response from the scattering crowd. Dad came up and put his arm around me.

"It was dumb, the whole damn thing. You knew it all along. Why did you play?"

"It was all I could do."

"I'm sorry, Johnny, really sorry. I had a hand in this, and I was wrong."

"It's okay, Dad. There are some things we just have to see for ourselves. That's why I went to Clarksdale."

The media awaited me. Crossing the parking lot, I spotted a few "Grab a Grand" badges among the discarded drink cups and popcorn funnels. The parents and girlfriends mingling near the locker room parted without looking at me. I almost collided with Principal MacMartin, who was in a rush. He said, "Well, Johnny, that was quite a ..." He couldn't figure out what it was, so he kept going.

A corner of the gym had been designated a press area. Hospitality tables bore soft drinks, a coffee urn, sandwich fixings, and homemade pies and cakes. The dazed media corps showed little interest in refreshments. A microphone sat on a table in front of rows of rented chairs. I wanted to get the interview over with quickly. Thirty or so reporters and several camera people faced me. From their blank expressions and sagging shoulders, I saw they had experienced enough of Spinkville and their profession on that night. Someone turned on a hot light at my back.

I answered the questions as best I could, although I didn't mention the slurs.

The red-haired reporter with the eerie white skin stood and said, "In a story published yesterday, you said you know what it's like to be black. What is it like?"

I thought about saying, "No comment," but I did not want to back away anymore from anything, even if I knew, as I surely did, that what I said would be used against me. So I spoke from the heart.

"Do you mean what it's like to be a black person in a white world? Then I guess it's having your individuality blurred because most whites are looking at you through their fear or guilt or envy. Black people may feel the same about whites, but it's blacks, not whites, who are reminded of their color so often. Their skin has consequences. Not having to think about your color… that's freedom."

Then a minister from down-state known for his devotion to publicity stepped to the front. He wore a teeshirt with the message, "It's a black thing. You wouldn't understand."

Michael Gaspeny

He said, "Young man, I'm proud of my color. What gives you the right to speak for me?"

"I'm not trying to speak for you. I answered a question based on my own experience."

The preacher sighed, and stared. "We have to learn to see beyond our experience," he admonished. "Now, will you join us in a prayer for racial understanding?"

"I don't know what you mean by racial understanding. Race doesn't exist unless it suits somebody's program."

"Race doesn't exist, you say? I repeat: Will you pray with us?"

"No, thank you. My every breath's a prayer."

I know all figures of speech are tricks, but I was being honest. I lived and breathed to be less stupid. I could say that much for myself.

That was my final statement. I left the tribunal and took the back way home in my socks, stripping my jersey, pads, and cleats and slinging them into the weeds.

You know what happens to information when it passes through a crowd. During the next week, the media commented more on their fabrications than what I had said. I was called a false prophet, a prayer-mocker, a bigot, and the product of indoctrination by Marxist professors whose summer class I had taken at the university. They repeatedly showed me on TV saying, "Race doesn't exist." As long as the analysts focused on me, they did not have to examine themselves.

In the realm of gratification, I had become a philanthropist. I had given the home crowd a spectacle that became a travesty and an opportunity for a good hand-washing. I had allowed Rae and Lee to remind me of my failings and feel good about themselves. I had permitted editorial writers and their audiences to feel enlightened. I had invigorated bigots on all sides. Coach Chuck Hurd gained an enhanced resume and his name in the record book next to an asterisk, but I knew that falling short of the fabled thousand would bother him until he died. As for me, I had received a severed foot in my front yard and the chance for a deeper inquiry into my character.

So Long

All winter, Dad sent college applications to me down in the Keys, but I never put a mark on one. During my blues course in Fayetteville and on all those game-day Saturdays there, I had seen student life. Now that I had visited Clarksdale, I felt too old for bull sessions, keg parties, and the great sex chase. I had learned that talking was dangerous, drinking led to more drinking, and Rae was the only girl I wanted. In Tavernier, at Coral Shores High School, I paid barely enough attention to pass. The teachers assumed I was dumb because I came from Arkansas, and I didn't show them otherwise.

For a long time, I fell asleep imagining Rae in my arms.

Then, in June, a card came from Mr. F in Paris, where he had taken his wife and Rae on vacation before moving her to Princeton. In a corner below his signature, his daughter had written, "Hi, Rae!" It was as if she were greeting herself. Her thoughtlessness made me angry. I had taken a barrage of hits last fall, some of which she had delivered. I remembered, "It's the girl who's supposed to tremble." I had been mocked by the media and forced to leave town. Decency would have led most people to wish me well or to write nothing. But the more I studied the curlicues in "Hi, Rae!" those syllables became an accidental act of mercy. Not even the most gaga lover could cling to fantasies in the face of Rae's disregard. I used the card to correct myself whenever I was moved to serve her tea again or recall that stunning afternoon in the amphitheater. "That's the girl who thinks nothing of you," I told myself. This refrain wasn't foolproof, but it shrank my desire.

Dad came down for graduation. Planning to skip the ceremony, I hadn't ordered a cap and gown. A believer in rituals, he drove to Miami and rented my regalia. I felt sorry for him after the ceremony because I had been such a zero at Coral Shores that as we passed through the crowd, most people had no idea who we were, and no one acknowledged us. It hurt Dad not to be known. He must have contrasted our quick exit with the triumphant graduation I would have had in Spinkville if I had never gone to Mississippi. Honors meant so much to him. Being my father's son, I, too, had once chased recognition. Back in my old room, I had drawers crammed with clippings from my football career and certificates of school, club, and church achievement. Now I wanted another way to measure my life. Dad talked about my future, but all I could say was that I wasn't coming home or going to college.

At first, the spiny Keys and their obsession with fishing had seemed so narrow that I felt jailed. But I had brought that confinement with me. Gradually, I took pleasure in the shifting water-colors of the sky, the ibises swinging their beaks as they gleaned the lawns in Uncle Roy's neighborhood, and the osprey nesting in the lights above the elementary school ball diamond. Sometimes wild parakeets flittered just above my head. It's nice to live in a place where you never know what you're going to see, especially after Spinkville. If it's possible to believe in a good afterlife, the Keys offer sketches of worlds to come. I told Dad I was going to stay for awhile.

Now when I close my eyes at night, the image of Rae dissolves into the birds I have seen that day, and my mind takes me to the wild bird center a couple of miles north of here. I've only been there two or three times, and I didn't stay long. This place where wounded birds mend had a strange effect on me: It was like seeing a person I wanted to know but felt unworthy to approach.

The trail starts in salt marsh under buttonwood trees and moves toward mangroves edging the Gulf. After the glare of the highway, the path seems dark until your eyes adjust to the red-tailed hawks, turkey vultures, and barred owls in cages. During the winter, strutting pelicans, tourists, and attendants crowd the splattered boardwalk. Free birds, some former patients at the refuge, roost on the railings and tin roofs of the bigger cages, occupied by roseate spoonbills, yellow-crowned night herons, and reddish egrets. You pass the profiles of cormorants with turquoise eyes so clear and bright that they seem more spirit than flesh.

The center is a resort for healthy birds, sailing and landing in every direction, preening in the trees and hunting in the ponds. Pelicans glide, vultures soar, gulls coast, and the wings of ibises scroll the air. It's easy to become hypnotized by the whirling spectacle and imagine yourself in paradise until you realize heaven contains no cages and some of the birds will never fly again. They were maimed by bullets, arrows, fish hooks, garbage, and violent weather. The closer you look, the more they resemble people you have known. But these creatures weren't harmed by pride or stupidity.

Michael Gaspeny

I had made my own snares, and I guess that no matter how perfect Rae seemed or what a swami Lee thought he was, they were trapped in the lounge of self-satisfaction. Lee's criticism of me applied to them, too. They couldn't see beyond themselves. Although I had lost the woman I loved, without ever standing a chance, in addition to my best friend, there was some consolation in trying to break the binds I created. Yes, I had the comfort of my music. But the blues had no patience with navel-gazing and drawn-out recoveries, and one morning not far away, it would kick me out on the highway again. Like Robert Johnson and Muddy Waters, I would wake up feeling around for my shoes.

From the middle of the trail at the wild bird center, you see the pale blue Florida Bay through the thicket of black mangrove. In an optical illusion, the water seems to stand, forming puzzle pieces outlined by the branches of the trees. It draws me along the final turnings of the boardwalk, past gold-footed snowy egrets stalking the pond, to what looks like a shabby beach. Drab water slides over crumbling coral, algae slicks, and claws of red mangrove. You wonder where those wandering red roots are going, out there in the muck, removed from the vegetation on shore. Below a gray sky, this beach is a lost-seeming place with no purpose except to give a sulfur-tainted hint of your own dead end.

But as the clouds and light shift, the water becomes a veil of the subtlest color, pale purple here and soft turquoise there, even a nearly invisible orange where the bottom is pasty mud. Under that spell, you realize that what's outside is also what's in, and if you contain the muck, you also carry the light.

The first time I saw that drab shore behind the bird center, I walked to the slow water in my flip-flops. Suddenly the gray light turned, and the veil spread. The beauty stunned me; I staggered. Something in the sea-weed jabbed my heel. I jumped. It looked like slimy claws, the whitish-gray shade of rot. I flashed back to Spinkville, the stink on my fingers, the paw on the lawn. For a flicker, I thought the demons of my last days at home had waited to re-claim me until exactly that moment when I felt a little freer. I wanted to run, but this time I forced myself to face what I had discovered, no matter how sickening. It was only snarled black mangrove ripped out by a storm, stewed in the bay, and slicked by dissolving jelly fish. When I seized the dripping roots, my relief crackled into laughter. I shook off the slime and hurled the debris into the water. I almost yelled, "That's the last claw!" but I didn't, because I don't talk trash anymore.

I knew from my music there would always be something lurking along the road out to grab and drag me down. But, with the

Michael Gaspeny

blues as my rock of faith, I thought I could keep my balance and move on, even if I was only stumbling in flip-flops. For the first time in the Keys, I felt some drive in my legs.

One stifling afternoon in July or August, when the tourists are gone and the beach is deserted, I'll set my tape player on the shore, and with Billie Holiday's voice easing me along, I'll walk into the water. After a long look west beyond the pelicans rocking in the waves, I'll imagine my decline as a floating cloud and watch as its shadow darkens the bay and the distant mangrove islands until it's gone. Then I'll fall down on my knees, raise up my right hand, and roll and tumble in the slow, sticky water. After my soak, I'll go up to the refuge and volunteer to clean cages and help with the birds until I'm ready to head to Helena or somewhere like it, because I don't think there's anything else for me to do. I can't know what I know and live a lie. That's not what my music's about.

Michael Gaspeny is the author of the novella in verse, *The Tyranny of Questions* (Unicorn Press) and the chapbooks *Re-Write Men* and *Vocation.* He has won the Randall Jarrell Poetry Competition and the O. Henry Festival Short Fiction Contest. His fiction has appeared in *storySouth, Brilliant Corners, The Greensboro Review,* and numerous anthologies. For hospice service, he received The (North Carolina) Governor's Award for Volunteer Excellence. He taught English for nearly four decades, mainly at Bennett College and High Point University, where he won the distinguished teaching award. A former reporter, Gaspeny covered the Arkansas Razorbacks and Bill Clinton's first campaign for national office. His stories about Clinton have often been quoted in works about the ex-president. A graduate of the MFA program in creative writing at the University of Arkansas, Gaspeny is married to the novelist and essayist Lee Zacharias. They have two sons, Al and Max.